By Heart

&

By Soul 

Hannah E. Carey

Published June 1st, 2023

Cover Design by Serenity Star Designs

Formatting by Serenity Star Press, LLC

Editing by West of Mars, LLC and The Editing Soprano

Dedication

To Rabiah,
For creating a safe haven for horses and humans.

Contents

1. Chapter 1 — 1

2. Chapter 2 — 9

3. Chapter 3 — 19

4. Chapter 4 — 27

5. Chapter 5 — 35

6. Chapter 6 — 47

7. Chapter 7 — 55

8. Chapter 8 — 67

9. Chapter 9 — 75

10. Glossary of Equestrian Terms — 83

11. Acknowledgements — 87

12. About The Author — 89

Chapter One

Nothing about my life was currently going to plan. As I pulled up to the green metal gate, I yawned so hard, my jaw popped. The headlights on my car illuminated the hand-carved wood sign that proudly let me know I'd arrived at Heart and Soul Ranch in Culpeper, Virginia. I should have been here three hours ago, but I'd gotten a flat tire just outside of Charlottesville and I'd had wait for AAA to come and switch my spare. And honestly, getting AAA had been sheer luck. When I'd called the number on the beaten-up plastic card I kept in my wallet, it turned out Aunt Glenda hadn't taken me off her policy yet, not that I expected that to last.

Note to self: Learn how to change a tire, I thought as I shifted the car into park and grabbed my phone off the passenger seat.

I could just add not being able to change a tire to the long list of life skills I was sadly lacking. After a car accident had killed both my parents when I was just six, my aunt Glenda had taken me in. But she had made it clear from the start that she didn't have time for me, leaving me to pretty much raise myself. And as soon as I'd turned eighteen, I'd gotten the hell away from her and the hell out of Atlanta. Glenda hadn't wanted me around and I hadn't wanted to stay and spend the rest of my life listening to her lectures about how I was never going to amount to anything.

As I pulled up a number on my phone, there was a flutter in my stomach. I'd wanted to make a good first impression on my new boss, Anita Lancaster. Arriving three hours late wasn't getting me off to a good start. Shaking my head, I hit the *send call* button. Hopefully Anita wouldn't be too mad.

"Hello?" Anita said when she picked up the phone.

"Hi, Miss Lancaster," I replied. "This is Meg Beckett. I just pulled in."

"Oh, wonderful. You were able to get roadside assistance, then?"

"Yes ma'am. I'm sorry it delayed me so much."

"There's nothing you can help about that. I'm just glad you made it safely. I'll be down in just a minute to open the gate. And Anita is fine, by the way."

"Okay. See you in a few minutes."

We hung up and I fidgeted with the steering wheel, my brief chat with Anita not doing much to settle my quivering stomach. The fact that she was so nice felt like it was making everything worse. I'd first seen her ad on an equestrian help wanted site a month ago and it had sounded perfect. The job as an assistant at Anita's rehab ranch included housing in the form of a small barn apartment, decent pay, and a small employee benefits package. I'd been looking for a full-time horse job since the moment I'd graduated high school back in May. I didn't want to spend the rest of my life working at a tiny little bagel shop in Atlanta and spending my weekends mucking stalls at Blue Moon Stables for crap pay and the hope I might be allowed to get on a horse.

While most of my graduating class had gone off to college, that wasn't an option for me. Glenda had made that perfectly clear. She didn't have the money to send me and I wasn't smart enough for scholarships. She was going to make me move out before the end of the year anyway, my supposed freeloading days over now that I was eighteen. Seeing Anita's job offer had felt like a sign from the universe or something. A way to prove to Glenda, and to myself, that I could amount to something.

The only problem was that I hadn't been entirely honest with Anita during my video call interview. I wasn't completely clueless about horses, but my experience was pretty limited. I'd cleaned stalls at Blue Moon on the weekends since I'd turned fifteen. Glenda hadn't been willing to pay for riding lessons, despite my love of horses, but I'd been determined to be around horses somehow. My stall mucking job had earned me occasional rides on an old school horse and, every once in a while, a lesson from the barn's trainer, Janet, but that was where my horse experience ended. I didn't know anything about running a barn or training a horse. I was banking everything on my ability to fake it until I made it. This job had gotten me away from Glenda and if I tried hard enough, maybe it could launch my future in the horse industry.

Pretty soon, headlights broke through the darkness as a large truck rolled down the gravel driveway, stopping on the other side of the gate. A figure popped out, one I soon recognized as Anita. She was dressed in a light windbreaker, jeans, and a pair of tall rubber boots. She unlatched the gate, waving at me before jumping back in her truck and moving the vehicle to the side of the driveway so I could pull in.

She got back out and latched the gate behind me before leading the way up the winding driveway. I followed behind her, wishing it wasn't pitch black so I could actually see the place. But even in the dark, I could pick out the shadows of trees and three-board fence. I knew from my interview and the ranch's website that it was located at the foothills of the Blue Ridge Mountains, a place I was hoping to visit at some point and take advantage of the endless, picturesque hiking.

Eventually, the driveway emptied into a gravel parking lot and I got my first glimpse at the large wooden barn that was going to be my new home. It was an older building, but it looked like it had been well-maintained. Anita parked her truck and I pulled in beside her before getting out of the car. The brisk wind made me shiver a little and I was glad I was wearing my hoodie. It was autumn right now, the first of September, and my first winter in the mountains was going to be a completely new experience.

"Do you need any help carrying your things?" Anita asked, coming over to join me at the trunk of my car.

"I don't have much. Thanks though," I replied, feeling a little self-conscious as I pulled out a ragged, faded duffle bag.

I didn't have a whole lot to call my own. My beat-up Honda that was practically on its last leg was probably the most valuable thing I owned. Glenda hadn't made much working as a hostess at a large chain diner and very little of her money had gone to me. Even with socking money away for a car since I was sixteen, the old beater was the best I'd been able to afford. I was probably lucky it had gotten me here at all,

I threw my duffle bag over my shoulder before grabbing my purse out of the front seat. Anita led the way across an open grassy area to the barn, pulling back one of the sliding doors so we could enter. The lights were on and I took a brief second to breathe in the comforting smell of horses, hay, and leather. I would make this work, one way or another. I was determined. That had to count for something, right?

"The stairs for the apartment are right this way," Anita said, motioning for me to follow her. "Just inside the tack room."

I trailed along behind her down the concrete aisle, the barn's setup throwing me slightly. I was used to long rows of single stalls, but this barn wasn't like that. On one side were what looked like spacious, oversized stalls, but the back walls were completely open, leading out into grassy fenced paddocks. On the other side were single stalls, but they were larger than what I was used to, the doors on the back sides of them hooked open to once again reveal more paddocks. And weirdly enough, I didn't see any horses. Not until we came to the last single stall.

A pretty dapple grey horse popped its head over the stall door, its ears pricked forward as it looked at me and Anita expectantly. Anita gave a light chuckle, pausing to rub the horse on the face. The horse's build reminded me of the fancy warmblood show hunters that had filled the stalls at Blue Moon. A brief glance at the brass plate on the stall door told me the horse's name: Winter Song. Fitting with her dappled coat.

"You've already gotten your night check hay, pretty girl," Anita said to the horse, taking a moment to peer into the stall. "And you haven't even finished it all."

"Where are the other horses?" I asked, readjusting the strap of my duffle bag, which had started to dig into my shoulder.

"They're out for the night," Anita answered. "Everyone is on twenty-four seven turnout here. Winter just arrived a few days ago so she's still in quarantine, but in the next week or so, she'll start going out with the others. With nice nights like this one, the horses tend to stay out in the fields, but they'll be back up in the barn for breakfast first thing in the morning."

I nodded, hoping my growing unease didn't show in my expression. Anita's explanation was another reminder of how out of my depth I was. I'd known from my interview that things at Heart and Soul were very different from what I was used to at Blue Moon, but it was starting to hit home just *how* different things were going to be. Turnout definitely hadn't been a priority at Blue Moon, and the horses had spent most of their time in their stalls. I'd only ever turned a horse out into a paddock twice, and that hadn't been a fun or easy job.

You'll figure it out, I reminded myself as Anita gave Winter one last scratch and we continued on our way into the tack room. I'd make this work. I had to. Glenda had made it pretty clear that when I'd left for Culpeper, I'd left for good. I wouldn't be welcome in her home any longer.

The tack room at least felt more familiar to me, with walls of bridles, saddles, pads, grooming kits, halters, lead lines, and more. I only saw one jumping saddle, the kind I had used at Blue Moon, but the dressage saddles that seemed to dominate the space didn't look all that different. The one Western saddle and the couple of rope halters were completely foreign to me, but there was always YouTube and Google.

I followed Anita up a narrow set of stairs and when we reached the top, she pushed open the door, giving me my first look at the apartment. It was honestly bigger than I'd expected. A half wall separated a living room from the small kitchen. It had been nicely furnished, the living room boasting a couch, two small chairs, a lamp, and a small TV. The kitchen even looked like it had a working stove.

"The bedroom and bathroom are back that way," Anita said, pointing down a short hallway. "There's linens and towels in the closet in the bathroom. If you need anything, just let me know."

"I will," I replied. "Thanks."

"I'll leave you to get settled," Anita said with a smile. "I'll see you bright and early tomorrow morning for feed up. I start at seven o'clock."

She let herself out and I let out a long breath before trudging back to the bedroom. Again, it was bigger than I'd expected. The queen-sized bed fit in the space comfortably, along with the dresser and nightstand. I dumped my bag on the ground near the foot of the bed. I'd unpack fully tomorrow, not that there was much to unpack. Briefly, I glanced out one of the two windows. I couldn't see much in the dark, but it looked like one of the pastures was right outside my window. That would be a nice view, seeing the horses every day.

Rummaging through my duffle, I found my toiletries and a pair of pajamas. I went over to the bathroom, taking a brief look around before brushing my teeth and getting ready for bed. Once back in the bedroom, I located an outlet, plugged in my phone charger, and crawled into bed. My phone definitely needed a charge before morning; it was already down to ten percent battery.

I yawned as I scrolled through social media for a few minutes, making a brief post that I'd made it safely to my destination. Not that there was anyone who would really care, but I could put the post up and pretend like someone did. Stifling a yawn, I placed my phone on the nightstand and nestled under the covers. My day would be starting bright and early; I needed what sleep I could get.

If I wanted to convince Anita I actually knew what I was doing when it came to being her assistant, I needed to be on my A game.

Chapter Two

My alarm went off at 6:00 a.m. I rolled out of bed with a groan, feeling like I did not get enough sleep. It was tempting to crawl back into the comfortable bed to try and catch a few more minutes of sleep, but I didn't need to start my first day off at my new job being late. There were horses waiting to be fed.

I shuffled to the bathroom, flipping on the lights on my way. Once I'd jumped in the shower, I went back to the bedroom to get dressed. Scrounging through my suitcase, I pulled out one of my nicer pairs of jeans and a collared shirt. I ended up tucking the shirt in and throwing on a belt, hoping maybe it would help me look a little more professional. My wardrobe was pretty slim. Hopefully now that I would be getting a decent paycheck, I'd be able to do something about that.

After I was dressed, I went into the kitchen, my stomach grumbling. I'd have to go grocery shopping sooner rather than later, but I at least still had a granola bar left from yesterday's drive. It didn't take long to find the coffee maker in the kitchen and I was ecstatic when I found coffee in one of the cabinets, tucked away with paper plates, paper cups, and plastic utensils.

Soon, I was nursing a cup of liquid energy, making my way down the stairs to the tack room. Taking in a deep breath of the blissful barn smell, I pulled my shoulders back at bit and strode out into the barn aisle. I'd landed this job and gotten the hell away from Glenda and Atlanta. This was going to be the start of better things; I was determined it would be.

By the time I reached the feed room, I'd finished my coffee and I tossed the empty cup into a tiny metal trash can near the door. Anita was bent over a large plastic trash can, scooping out various horse feeds and dumping them into large rubber pans spread out across the floor. My stomach churned a little as I watched her. I could count on one hand the number of times I'd fed the horses at Blue Moon and I definitely had never mixed a horse's feed ration all by myself. *You'll figure it out,* I told myself. *It can't be that hard.* Or so I hoped.

"Good morning," I told Anita, mustering up what I hoped was a confident smile.

"Good morning," she replied, returning my smile with one of her own. "How did you sleep? I see you found the coffee."

"I slept great, thanks. And thanks for the coffee. I'll probably try and hit the grocery store at some point today."

"Let me know when you're headed out and I can give you directions," Anita said. "Morning chores are pretty simple. The horses get brought out of the run-ins and put into their stalls to eat. I'm not haying much right now with the pastures still being good, but there is some hay to throw. We'll do a quick pick of the run-ins and stalls, throw some hay, make sure everyone has water, turn them back out, and then tidy things up."

I nodded, the churning in my stomach growing with each word she spoke. This was completely different from how things had been done at Blue Moon. I could only hope I wouldn't look like a total idiot by the end of the morning.

Anita motioned me over and I joined her in front of the row of plastic trash cans. To my relief, all of the feeding instructions were written on a dry erase board that was nailed to the wall over top the cans of feed. I could follow instructions. Or, at least I hoped I could. They were way more detailed and extensive than I was expecting.

I helped Anita dump the dry pellets, some green, some tan, and some almost black, into the rubber pans. Then we added in supplements. That part was more than a little confusing considering there were both dry supplements and liquid ones, but the list was also at least written down on the dry erase board. Once the feed was prepared, we carried the pans to the wash stall. I helped Anita set them out in a specific order and she informed me we'd wet them before feeding them to the horses to prevent them from choking and keep them better hydrated. Another thing I had definitely not done before at Blue Moon.

"Ready to go get some horses?" she asked after we soaked the last of the feed down with the hose.

"Definitely," I replied. I'd handled and led horses before. That would be way easier than trying to keep everyone's feed straight.

Anita led the way to the first run-in which, unlike last night, was filled with horses. Three of them—a handsome, leggy white grey, a long-maned chestnut, and a petite little chestnut and white paint—huddled near the door, letting out whinnies and nickers when they saw us approaching. Humans were clearly synonymous with food to them at this time of day.

"These guys are pretty easy. They're all my personal horses. The other four horses are client horses," Anita said, passing me one of the halters hanging outside the stall. "I'll let you get Fuego. He goes in the stall next to Winter."

I nodded, feeling a little boost of confidence as I took the halter and lead. I knew how to do this.

"I do have a specific way I like them haltered," Anita continued, unlatching the door. "I'll show you with Smoke."

My stomach flip-flopped again. So much for thinking this would be something I was good at. I followed her into the stall and over to the lanky grey. Anita undid the halter by unbuckling the crownpiece, then showed me how she slipped it onto the gelding's face. I watched her closely, determined not to mess this up, but when I walked over to the chestnut, Fuego, and began to put his halter on, I was still left fumbling. I gritted my teeth as I fought with the nylon straps, my heart pounding and my skin hot with embarrassment. This was a simple task I *should* have been able to do.

"You'll have it straight in a few days," Anita told me when I finally buckled the halter in place. "It just takes practice."

My cheeks were still flushed, but I mumbled an acknowledgement.

We led the horses out into the aisleway and I tried to focus on the soothing sound of the steady clop of their hooves on the concrete instead of my mounting incompetence. There was a different cadence to the hoof falls than I was used to and when I walked Fuego into his stall, I noticed there weren't any metal shoes on his hooves. *Right,* I reminded myself. *Anita said she rarely uses shoes; the horses are barefoot.* I remembered that from the interview. I'd never taken care of a barefoot horse before, but it couldn't be too hard, right?

Once Fuego and Smoke were closed in their stalls, we returned to the first run-in. Anita had me get Esperanza, the lone remaining paint mare, myself, though she was there to help. Which, it turned out, was a good thing. Not only was I still struggling with haltering the mare in the way she had instructed me to, Esperanza was much more skittish than Fuego had been. I finally got the lavender halter clipped in place, but I was feeling pretty well like a failure as I led the mare out of the run-in, purposefully not meeting Anita's gaze.

"She hasn't been here long," Anita said, walking down the aisleway on the other side of the mare. "Almost two months. I don't normally get much on the ones that come from auction, though it seems like this girl was passed around a lot. I can only imagine what her life was like before she ended up at the auction house. She was in rough shape."

I felt a twinge of sympathy for the skittish mare; it wasn't easy being taken away from everything you knew. Once the mare was in her stall, we went to the second run-in and fetched the last four horses. Anita passed on little tidbits about each horse as we moved them over to their stalls, and I tried to file away as much information as I could. After all, I was going to be expected to help take care of this little herd of eight.

The chestnut Thoroughbred mare, Storm Hart, was here because she'd become difficult to mount, while the black Warmblood gelding, Talisman, was here because of something called kissing spines. The two Welsh ponies, Olaf and Elsa, belonged to twin sisters, but had both come to Heart and Soul for training issues. Olaf struggled with bucking at the canter and Elsa was difficult for her young rider to handle, bolting and pulling away on the ground, along with refusing to stand still when tied. I didn't understand everything Anita was telling me, but I still tried to pay close attention. I'd research and look up what I could remember later.

Once the horses were in their stalls and fed, it was time to pick the large run-ins. Anita took one while I took the other. As I gripped the pitchfork in hand and began cleaning out the dirty bedding, I allowed myself a quiet sigh of relief. *This* I knew how to do. And compared to the small stalls at Blue Moon where the horses stayed in twenty to twenty-three hours a day, cleaning the stalls and run-ins at Heart and Soul was a breeze.

"Nicely done," Anita said, poking her head into the run-in I was working in just as I finished up spreading the last of the fresh bedding. "The hay nets just need one pad of hay each in them. They're hung on the wall with clips, so they're easy to pull down. Just make sure you re-clip everything to the baling twine and not the actual rings for safety when you hang them back up."

I nodded, wiping a hand on the leg of my jeans as my palms grew clammy again. I didn't have the first clue how much a *pad* of hay was. And I couldn't ask. Not without looking like an idiot. Instead, I walked over to where the hay nets had been hung on the run-in walls. Not that I had any real experience with those either. At Blue Moon, I'd seen them put into the horse trailers when the horses traveled, but that was it.

With a little difficulty, I pulled all four of the dark purple and maroon nets down from the walls. Throwing the four nets over my shoulder, I followed Anita's directions to the hay room. *This can't be this hard,* I told myself, taking a deep breath as I entered the small open bay that was stacked high with bales of sweet-smelling grass hay. I dumped the empty nets onto one of the empty pallets, staring with trepidation at an already opened hay bale. I could just eyeball it, right? Make an educated guess based on how much hay I'd seen put in the stalls at Blue Moon?

Allowing myself a quiet groan, I started poking around in the open bale. It looked like it was divided into chunks, but how the heck was I supposed to know how many of these chunks was the equivalent of a pad? Hell, they weren't all even the same size. *Why call them pads, anyway,* I grumbled, finally settling on a chunk of hay that seemed like it was close to the right amount.

I pulled it apart from the rest of the bale, only to realize a few moments later that that was the least of my problems. I was pretty sure hay nets were demons in disguise, because I could not manage to get the hay inside the nets. I was starting to sweat from the sheer effort of fighting with the uncooperative nets. At one point, I rolled up my long sleeves to my elbows to try and cool off, only to end up with tiny bits of itching hay all over my skin.

"Everything going okay in here?" Anita asked.

I started when I heard her, dropping both the hay and the net I was wrestling with onto the rubber-matted floor. I couldn't stop myself from cursing under my breath as I scrambled to pick everything up, my face flushing yet again.

"I, ah, I'm kind of having a hard time with the nets," I said, barely able to keep myself from cringing. At this rate, I'd barely be able to make it a whole week before she saw right through me. "We didn't have them at my old barn."

"They are a bit of a pain, even if they do keep the horses from eating too quickly," Anita replied with a good-natured smile but that smile faded when she took a few steps forward and got a better look at the mess I'd made.

"Oh, it's only one pad each per net," she said with a frown. "You don't need to put half the bale in them."

My flush deepened and I winced. I wished I could melt right into the floor. Clearly, I had not guessed correctly at all on the amount of hay.

"Here," Anita said, grabbing one of the empty nets and a chunk of hay. "I'll show you a few tricks that'll help."

I paid close attention to what she was doing, especially how much hay she was gathering for each net, and with her help, the nets—which I still wasn't fully convinced weren't demon spawn in disguise—were filled. But by the time we left the hay room behind, the re-filled, and noticeably heavier, nets once again slung over my shoulder, my pulse had ticked up again. I couldn't make another mistake this morning. If I lost this job, I didn't have another one waiting in the wings.

We soon finished with the run-ins and when the horses were done eating, we turned them back out in their small herds. I was feeling a little less intimidated by Anita's haltering method by the time we turned the last horse out, though I was glad she'd handled the training horses who'd needed to be led in and out in rope halters. I'd never seen a halter like that in my life and I was not up for putting on a halter that required tying knots when I was barely handling buckles.

"That's all there is for morning chores," Anita said as the two of us lingered outside the feed room. "It's a little more involved depending on the time of year or if there's a horse who needs medical care, but it's pretty straightforward. I thought today I'd give you the rest of the morning and afternoon off to get settled, go to the store, things like that. I'll start showing you the grooming and basic groundwork routines for the horses tomorrow."

Groundwork—another thing I didn't have a clue about. At Blue Moon, the focus had been on riding the horses. I'd seen the naughty ones lunged, but that was about the extent of my groundwork experience. At Heart and Soul, however, Anita had made it clear that things like groundwork were a big deal. And whether I thought it was a waste of time or not, it was part of the job. And tonight, I was having a serious date with some YouTube videos because tomorrow I was apparently getting fully thrown in the deep end.

"That sounds great," I said, plastering on what I hoped was a convincing smile. "Would it be possible to get those directions to the grocery store from you? I think I'd rather go earlier in the day."

I didn't have much in the way of cash after my trip down, but I at least should be able to get some bare bones basics to tide me over until I got my first paycheck at the end of the week.

"Of course," Anita replied.

I texted myself the directions Anita gave me for the closest grocery store, which it turned out was a ten-mile drive, then headed back upstairs. Once I was in the privacy of the apartment, I let out a loud groan, rubbing my forehead. I was so, so out of my depth here, it wasn't even funny. And Anita's kindness was only making me feel worse. I *should* tell her the truth—that I had led her to believe I was more experienced than I was—but if I did, then what? She'd probably kick me out and I wouldn't have anyplace to go. Not to mention that my horse dreams would be toast and I would have just proved Glenda right in her assertion that I was never going to amount to anything. No, telling the truth wasn't an option. I would have to do some serious homework and do my darnedest to appear as confident as possible. I *had* to pull this off.

Chapter Three

By the end of the week, I was starting to feel more confident with the daily ranch chores and the following Friday night, I was left to do night check on my own for the first time. Anita's trust felt huge and was a much needed boost to my confidence. She had also given me an additional task on top of regular chores that I was more than happy to do. I needed to give Winter Song a good, thorough grooming.

Night check chores were easy, consisting of making sure the horses had water, tossing extra hay if needed, and giving a third meal of the day to Anita's ex-racehorse, Smoke, to help him keep a good weight. As I finished topping the waters in the second run-in, I let my gaze drift to the large paddocks, which I'd learned let out into even larger pastures on the back side of the barn. The horses were out grazing, enjoying the cool fall evening. The kaleidoscope of their coat colors set against the red and gold trees, with the ever-present Blue Ridge in the backdrop, was a breathtaking sight I wasn't sure I'd ever get tired of looking at. There was enough of a nip in the air that I was glad I'd thrown on a sweatshirt before coming downstairs, and the long shadows from the setting sun hinted at the shorter days that were soon headed our way.

Once I was finished topping the water buckets off, I coiled the hose back up in the wash stall, then went to go check on Smoke. The gelding was nose deep in his rubber feed pan, munching away, but he was almost done with his grain ration. I hung out outside the stall, leaning against the wall and pulling my phone out of my pocket while I waited. As I scrolled social media, I couldn't help but feel a slight twinge in my chest at the lack of notifications. I hadn't been very good at making friends in Atlanta. I'd always gotten along better with animals than people. They didn't judge, didn't look at me as the girl whose parents had died.

I'd spent years pretending the loneliness didn't bother me, but if I was truly honest with myself, it did. Sometimes, I wondered if anyone really cared. Allowing myself a small sigh, I tucked my phone back in my back pocket. I hadn't expected anyone to check in on me, not even Glenda, but for some stupid reason, the fact that I'd left Atlanta and not a single person gave a damn still hurt.

Smoke popped his head over the door, his ears swiveling toward me as he looked at me expectantly. I couldn't help but smile. At least there were always horses. I grabbed his halter off the hook outside the stall, opting for the leather halter instead of the rope one. I still hadn't mastered those things yet and I honestly didn't feel at all confident putting one on without Anita nearby.

Smoke stood quietly while I got the halter over his head, still fumbling a bit with Anita's technique, though after almost two weeks, I was starting to get the hang of it. Leading Smoke out of the stall, I put him back in the run-in, the gelding wandering off to go graze outside in the cool night air with the rest of the herd.

I walked back to the tack room, fetching Winter's grooming box. I'd groomed the mare once already under Anita's supervision and it had felt good to have her assign me the task to do on my own. I'd messed up more times than I would have liked to since I'd gotten here, but outside of a few strange looks here and there, Anita had been kind about everything. More than once, I wondered if she'd figured out that I wasn't as experienced as I'd claimed by the way she'd divided up tasks between us, but at least she hadn't fired me or yelled at me—yet. At times, her patience kind of unnerved me; I wasn't used to it. Glenda had been a yeller, and so had Janet, the head trainer at Blue Moon.

Before letting myself into Winter's stall, I grabbed her purple halter. Anita had wanted me to groom the mare in the stall, as she was still working on Winter's tying skills. Winter was munching on the hay in her hay net in the far corner, briefly turning her head back to look at me as I closed the stall door.

"Hi, sweet girl," I said, walking over.

I had a little bit of a hard time getting Winter to leave the hay long enough for me to put the halter on, but Anita had shown me a few tips and tricks. Once the halter was snugly on Winter's face, I pulled a treat out of my pocket. Careful to make sure I paid attention to my timing in order to offer the reward at the exact right moment, I waited until Winter stood quietly next to me, without invading my space, before giving it to her. I wasn't really used to using treats with horses, but it was something Anita did as a part of the training program.

There was a structure and a clear method behind every single interaction with horses at the ranch, one that Anita was strict about being followed in the interest of being fair and clear to the horses. I'd been a little skeptical the first week or so, but slowly, I was starting to see that despite Anita's often unorthodox methods, they did work, and bit by bit, I was gleaning the logic and process that laid behind her system. The horses at Heart and Soul wanted to be with humans, associating them with good things, and there was a calm confidence to their demeanors that made them a joy to be around, as if they were comfortable in their own skins. Anita had warned me not all of the horses arrived that way, but that was always her goal by the time they left the ranch.

As Winter continued to eat her hay, I got to work on getting her groomed. At some point today, she had gone out in her paddock and rolled, getting dirt and bits of dried mud all over her dappled grey coat. I set to work with a curry comb, knocking off the worst of the mess with each circular stroke. Winter seemed content to eat while I worked, occasionally flicking an ear back at me every now and then.

Anita had told me a little bit of the mare's story. The beautiful Hanoverian mare had been a show hunter for the first few years of her life, then retired early due to an injury to her suspensory ligament. She'd then been sent off to be a broodmare, but unfortunately for her, the breeding farm hadn't been the most reputable. Winter, along with fifteen other mares, had eventually been seized and pulled by the local county animal control due to neglect.

After Anita had adopted Winter from Animal Control, she had brought the mare to Heart and Soul. Winter still had some weight to gain, as well as some healing to do, and the verdict was still out on whether or not Winter would be able to return to light riding, but regardless of the outcome, Anita was willing to keep her. Her story, Anita had said, was one of the lucky ones, with a happy ending. Not all horses were nearly as lucky. As I switched from the rubber curry to a wood-backed stiff brush, I silently hoped the mare's life was nothing but good things from here on out; she'd been through a lot in her six years of life.

I hummed quietly to myself as I continued to work. There had always been something cathartic about grooming a horse and I cherished every moment that passed in the quiet, peaceful barn. One thing I had noticed over the past few days that I had come to really love was how quiet and peaceful Anita kept the ranch. She'd said she always wanted this to be a calming place for people and horses, and you could feel it. Not that everything went perfectly every day; it didn't, but I was starting to think Anita's intention for this place always being a safe haven really did make a difference. It was certainly different than Blue Moon, where things had always been rushed, harried, agitated, and you never quite knew when you were going to get yelled at next. Even the horses had been perpetually cranky there.

It took a while to get Winter truly clean, but I didn't mind. This was where I was happiest, in the presence of a horse. I was working on Winter's mane, the rest of her body now sparkling, when Esperanza wandered into the run-in on the other side of the aisleway. Winter turned her head toward the other mare, letting out a soft nicker. Esperanza nickered back, looking at Winter with her ears pricked for a few seconds before she went over to one of the refilled hay nets and started chowing down.

Winter watched the other horse intently and I stroked her neck. "You're ready for friends, aren't you?"

Anita had mentioned during chores this morning that she planned to turn Winter out with Fuego this weekend, the chestnut gelding apparently the ranch's goodwill ambassador when it came to meeting new horses. Once they'd had a few days to get to know one another, Winter would then get to go out with the rest of the herd.

Winter nickered at Esperanza again and I scratched her neck. "I think you're going to be in luck. Anita said that's the herd she's going to try you in first. Hopefully, they'll be nice and you'll all get along. Maybe you'll get to have Esperanza for a friend."

I was pretty sure to anyone watching, I'd look crazy for talking to a horse, but all you had to do was spend time around them to realize they were intelligent beings with their own lives and relationships. And Anita had made a comment to me earlier this week that while horses didn't exactly understand our words, they could understand our intentions; there was something that often came out in the way we talked to them. I was taking her word on that one and hoping she wouldn't think I was crazy if she walked in on me talking to any of the horses while I worked.

After watching Esperanza for a few moments, Winter let out a low snort and returned to her own hay. I resumed brushing her mane, working out the snarls and tangles before moving back to her tail, trying not to dwell on the fact that while Winter would be getting her own friends soon, I still didn't have any real meaningful friends in my life.

Telling myself I didn't need them was starting to feel a little hollow, even if I didn't want to admit that out loud. *But what's the point?* I thought, taking some of my frustration out on a particularly gnarly knot in Winter's tail. *You always end up disappointed by people anyway.* I was pretty used to people failing me, and it just seemed easier to cling to my self-reliance. But the longer I spent around Anita, in this place, far away from Glenda and my past in Atlanta, I caught myself wanting things I'd never really wanted before. Things like a family, and friends, and a place to call home. Yet at the same time, all of this was on a knife's edge, ready to come crumbling down if Anita figured out how much I'd lied to her. My stomach clenched and I bit my lip. I had to remember that I couldn't get too comfortable here. That would only make things hurt all the more if I lost it all.

Chapter Four

IT WAS A KNOT. How difficult could it be to tie a knot? I stared at the rope halter, sagging haphazardly on Fuego's head, as frustration welled up inside me. Two weeks into my job at Heart and Soul and I'd been just starting to feel like I was getting the hang of things—until today.

I whipped my phone out of my back pocket, Fuego letting out a long-suffering sigh as I checked the time. I was supposed to be in the arena with the gelding in five minutes for my first lesson with Anita and I couldn't even get this damn halter on right. Barely stifling a groan, I drew my shoulders back, determined to make it work. Part of my contract at Heart and Soul included two lessons a month from Anita and I didn't need to make an idiot of myself at my very first one.

Anita had shown me more than once how to tie the knot that held the halter in place, and yet somehow, I always messed it up. I'd spent last night watching YouTube videos on how to do it but this morning when I'd been confronted with putting on Fuego's navy blue rope halter, I'd just been left fumbling. Why, oh why, couldn't Anita just use the leather halters for groundwork? Sure, she'd told me all about how when she was training, she preferred the feel of the rope halters and the special rope leads that tied on instead of having a snap, but these things just seemed like way too much work to me.

It's sink or swim, I reminded myself as I made my sixth attempt at tying the halter. This time it at least looked mostly right and I remembered to tuck in the little bit of extra rope so that it wouldn't swing around near Fuego's eye. Buckling on my helmet, the one piece of horse equipment I owned outside my cracked and worn leather paddock boots, I led Fuego out of the barn.

Fuego walked along quietly beside me as we walked the short distance down the gravel path to the large riding arena, but even with his calm demeanor, by the time we reached the gate, my stomach was a quiver of knots. I had never done any sort of groundwork at Blue Moon. I didn't even really know what it was outside of lunging, and I could count on one hand the number of times I'd seen that done. Not to mention that I didn't think lunging was something we were going to be doing today. I'd watched Anita work with the horses enough to figure that out.

In all honesty, a lot of Anita's methods seemed a little strange. I was warming up to them, slowly, but I was used to seeing a lot more action and drama when it came to horse training. Watching Anita was more like watching paint dry. She was slow, methodical, and a lot of the time, I wondered if anything at all was even happening. It definitely wasn't the Hollywood version of a horse whisperer.

Once I led Fuego into the area, we traipsed across the bluestone and sand ring to join Anita, who stood near a couple of large plastic orange cones. They'd been arranged into a large square and my stomach churned again. I hoped I wasn't supposed to know what in the hell I was supposed to do with those.

"We're just going to get started with some basic things today," Anita said with a smile, coming over to scratch Fuego's neck.

I really wanted to tell her that her cone maze looked anything but basic, but I couldn't do that without admitting my lies. Anita's gaze went to the rope halter and I tensed, barely suppressing a wince when she gave a slight frown.

"Almost," she said, smoothing her features as she undid the halter. "The knot is right. You just need to loop it around the bottom part, not the top; otherwise it'll work its way loose. Like this."

She tied the halter back up with practiced ease.

"Sorry," I said, my cheeks flushing.

"Mistakes happen. And tying rope halters takes practice. Good job remembering to tuck the extra bit in away from his eye."

Well, I'd gotten one thing right, at least. Hopefully that counted for something.

She cast me a sidelong glance, tilting her head ever so slightly, and I swore, she was looking right through me. "This is all a bit different than it was at your old barn in Atlanta, isn't it?"

My face flushed and I made a small circle in the sand with the toe of my boot, the state of the cracked leather only making me feel more self-conscious. "Yeah… yeah, it's been different here."

I regretted the words as soon as I said them, swallowing hard. Had I seriously just admitted that I was a fraud? *Maybe it will be for the best,* I thought, trying to ignore the sweat that was beginning to build on my palms. *Maybe she'll think you're just having a little bit of culture shock instead of being completely incompetent.*

"We'll get you caught up," Anita said, taking a few steps back. "First things first, I want to talk a little bit about the horse's center of gravity."

I couldn't keep my eyes from widening. Now I *knew* I was out of my depth. Hoping my cluelessness didn't show on my face, I tried to soak in every word Anita said as she showed me where a horse's center of gravity was, using Fuego to demonstrate, and how easily a horse's balance could get thrown off because of their lack of collarbone.

"Certainly not always, but a lot of behavioral issues end up being balance issues. That being said, there's a lot of things we can do to address the balance and the behavior," Anita said as she finished up her lecture. "So today, I want to show you some simple exercises to get you started."

I nodded, my trepidation leaving me with a dry mouth.

"You'll have it pretty easy today," Anita said as I led Fuego over to the center of the cones. "Fuego knows this stuff pretty well. It's tricker with a horse who doesn't really know what you're asking."

We started with asking Fuego to move his shoulders to the left and right, and quite frankly, I felt like an idiot. It had sounded simple enough when Anita had given me the instructions, but it quickly became apparent to me that Anita was all about the details.

"Slower," Anita called, standing a few feet away to give Fuego and me space to work. "You want to give him time to respond to the softer cue. If you start with heavy, all you'll ever get is heavy. Give him time to think."

I blew out a long breath, starting the whole sequence of cues again and applying less pressure to Fuego's shoulder and neck as I asked him to step his front legs over.

"Soften your shoulders," Anita said. "He's going to mirror you and feel that tension in your body. If he's tight, it will make it all the harder for him to shift his weight."

I rolled my shoulders, trying to do as she said, though it wasn't easy with the anxiety that kept my stomach fluttering. If I epically failed in this lesson, would that be the thing that caused her to fire me?

"And breathe." Out of the corner of my eye, I saw a hint of a smile on Anita's face. "You can't learn it all in one day, and no one expects you to. Just be in this moment; don't overthink it. Feel his body and yours."

I took a couple deep breaths, trying to find that elusive place of calm that Anita seemed to always operate from when she was around the horses. Fuego's ears flicked a few times and it seemed as if he wasn't bracing against me quite as much as before. Two more deep breaths followed and then it happened. Fuego stepped away, moving his shoulders to the right. I bit my lip, suppressing the smile that wanted to break out. Okay, maybe that *was* a little cool. For a moment, it was like Fuego had read my thoughts, even though I knew he'd really just been responding to my cues, thanks to Anita's training. Still, the feeling had been a little addictive.

"Very good!" Anita called. "Go ahead and use a treat to mark that response."

I pulled a training treat out of my pocket, making sure the gelding wasn't mugging me before giving it him.

"Now, when you start working with the training horses, you'll find a lot of them will struggle with this exercise in that they'll want to just keep moving forward instead of moving away because they're unbalanced, have a pattern of bracing, or they just don't understand what you're asking them to do. That's part of why I want to show you the backing; it's a good tool to have up your sleeves with a horse who's heavy and braced their shoulders."

Anita walked back over, showing me how to ask Fuego to back up by cueing him with the halter or with a hand on his chest. She then had me practice asking him to back between sets of cones, first rewarding the gelding when he just gave a step or two, then holding the reward until he backed all the way between the obstacles.

"There," Anita said, nodding in approval as I brought Fuego to a stop. "That was softer that time, wasn't it? It took less."

I nodded, unable to keep myself from smiling. Maybe this stuff wasn't as boring as I'd first thought.

"I think that's a good place to stop for the both of you for today," Anita said. "You can practice what we worked on with him in between now and your next lesson. I'd recommend it, really. The more practice you get, the better your timing will get and the better you'll get at reading the horses."

"I definitely will," I told her. As much as I could. I knew I was behind the curve here; I'd do anything I could to catch up.

"And don't stress too much over getting everything perfect right away. It will come. When most new clients get here, most of them don't have a whole lot of experience with groundwork. It's something that improves the more you practice. Just like riding."

The words soothed me a little. Maybe I didn't have to be perfect at everything in order to keep this job. Anita led the way back to the barn, Fuego and I following behind her. By the time I had brushed the gelding down and turned him back out in his run, the tightness in my chest had been replaced by a lighter feeling. Maybe, just maybe, I *could* get the hang of this. I'd keep researching everything I could find on horse care and keep practicing with Fuego. I hadn't had a future when I'd left Atlanta, but maybe I really did have one here.

Chapter Five

RIDING IN ANITA'S TRUCK was definitely different than riding in my beat-up old Honda, and not just because of the loud hum of the diesel engine. While the outside of the maroon Ford F-250, with the heart-shaped ranch logo made up of horse heads, was practically pristine, the inside was a little dirty and smelled strongly of hay and horse. Bits of baling twine were tied up on the floor at my feet and a lone lead rope had been thrown up on the dashboard. I fidgeted with the strap of my seat belt as the truck rumbled down the winding country road, hoping I didn't look as nervous as I felt, while Anita hummed to a country tune playing on the radio.

She'd wanted me to come with her to the clinic today at Haven Hills Equestrian Center, saying it would be good for me to make connections with some of the local horse people, as well as be able to watch the clinic as an auditor and pick up some extra education. That part I was looking forward to, even if the topic of the clinic, body awareness for jumping, was completely foreign to me. Outside the passenger's seat window, I watched as we passed by rolling green hills, some of them dotted with various crops while others boasted the clean lines of wood board fence that enclosed horses—or the occasional cow. It would be a beautiful crisp fall day to be outside, especially after the last few days of rain.

"Ellen's daughter is the same age you are," Anita said, drawing my attention back to her. "Sierra is riding first thing this morning, but she'll be auditing the rest of the day afterward."

I swallowed hard and tried to force a weak smile. *This* was what I was nervous about. From the little bits Anita had told me, Sierra had grown up on her family's farm and had been around horses basically since she was born. Would she take one look at me and be able to tell I was completely clueless? Or even worse, would she go and tell Anita? I'd wished there'd been an easy way out of this, but Anita had been insistent. I'd gotten the vibe that she thought this would be a good opportunity for me to get off the ranch and make some friends. The thing was, I didn't need friends; not really.

When we pulled into a gravel driveway, my stomach churned, leaving me half-wondering if I was going to be forced to give up the granola bar I'd scarfed down for breakfast. The green and white sign at the start of the driveway had a large silhouette of a jumping horse, and the words *Haven Hills Equestrian Center* were written in a scrawling script. It didn't take long to figure out that Haven Hills was bigger than Heart and Soul. After we passed a couple of large pastures and drove up to a gravel parking lot in front of a large green and white barn, I spied a matching green and white indoor arena. And behind that was a jumping ring along with what I thought looked like a small dressage ring. I was *so* out of my league here.

Anita put the truck in park and I clambered out behind her, my palms sweaty as I shoved my hands in my back pockets. I followed as Anita led the way to the indoor arena, dodging small puddles as we went. Riding indoors definitely seemed a smart move after last night's particularly heavy rainstorm. Once we reached the indoor, we joined the rest of the spectators in a small corner that had been sectioned off with ground poles and a few jump standards. Thankfully there were still a few empty seats.

Anita sat down in an empty chair next to an older red-haired woman and I sat down beside her. In the arena, a girl about my age was trotting around on a tall bay horse; a Thoroughbred, if I had to guess. The horse's light-colored tack looked good against his dark brown coat and his rider posted the trot with ease in her spotless jumping saddle. The clinician was in the middle of the arena, calling out instructions to the pair.

"So glad you could make it," the stranger sitting next to Anita said quietly.

"Me too," Anita replied. "Ellen, this is my new assistant, Meg. Meg, this is Ellen MacFarlane."

MacFarlane. Right; the MacFarlane family owned Haven Hills.

"Nice to meet you," I told Ellen, mustering up a smile.

"Nice to meet you as well, Meg," Ellen replied. "It's good that Anita has some help at the ranch. Sierra's riding, but once she's done, y'all can get to know one another."

I nodded, my gaze straying back to the rider in the arena, who was now trotting her horse over a set of ground poles. That had to be Sierra then and quite frankly, she was *good.* She didn't have the tall, slender build that seemed to so often be favored in riding, but she communicated with her mount with the subtlest of cues as they glided around the arena. Her hair was tucked under her black helmet, but it looked to be the same red as her mom's, and as she smoothly came around and trotted over the poles again in an effortless two-point jumping position, I found myself even more nervous that this girl would know I was faking it in two seconds flat.

Trying to shove aside my worries, I forced myself to focus on what the clinician was saying. I was determined to learn something today. I hadn't really gotten to jump at Blue Moon. With as sporadic as my riding time and rare lessons had been, I had only gone over ground poles, but maybe I would be able to learn more about jumping through Anita. I didn't know if jumping was necessarily my passion—I'd been pretty drawn to the bits of dressage I'd seen Anita doing with the horses over the last three weeks—but I was determined to learn as much as I could at this job.

The clinician had Sierra go over the ground poles a few more times, correcting and adjusting Sierra's position before having the pair move on to a few small jumps at the other end of the ring. I didn't understand entirely what was going on, but I thought I was getting the gist of it. The horse would move and respond better if Sierra kept her body in balance with the horse's movements. It was different than the handful of jumping lessons I'd watched at Blue Moon, more focused on correcting the rider than correcting the horse, but it did seem to work. Sierra and her gelding were jumping more smoothly at the end of their ride than at the beginning. Soon, Sierra's session came to an end and she dismounted, leading her horse out of the arena while a new rider came in, this time a woman who looked to be in her mid-forties with a cute little chestnut Quarter Horse. The breed of the horse was pretty obvious with its short, stocky build and large hindquarters.

"Let's go meet Sierra," Anita said, motioning for me to get up.

"She'll be in the barn with Wings," Ellen said. "This is one of my clients, so I'm going to stay for right now."

"Of course," Anita replied. "We'll be back in a bit."

I followed Anita out of the arena, my stomach churning more with every step we took toward the green and white barn. Sierra was clearly so much more experienced than I was and what if she didn't even like me? I shoved my hands in my pockets again, my mouth dry as Anita and I walked across the grassy open area between the barn and the indoor arena. We passed a couple of parked horse trailers, where riders were readying their mounts. One horse in particular caught my eye, a flashy black with four white stockings, a broad blaze, and one blue eye. He was huge, powerfully built, and even I could tell he was likely expensively bred.

A guy a little older than me was holding him while he danced around at the end of the lead line, clearly excited by his current situation. The guy holding him didn't look at all happy with the horse's behavior, snapping at him that he needed to stop acting up. At the other end of the trailer, a girl around my age was zipping on a pair of chocolate-colored tall boots, glancing nervously at the fractious horse. Anita called for me to keep up and a few moments later, we stepped into the barn aisleway. Anita led us past the rows of stalls, eventually stopping in front of Sierra's gelding. The horse was tied and Sierra was removing his tack.

"Wings looks good, Sierra," Anita said.

"Thanks," Sierra replied, beaming as she removed a hunter green saddle pad from Wings' back. "Mom had me take a few steps back with him this summer and I honestly think it's been one of the best things for him."

"Sometimes we have to take a few steps back in order to move forward again." Anita gestured to me. "This is my new assistant, Meg. Meg, this is Sierra MacFarlane. Sierra, your mom and I thought since you girls are the same age, you could show Meg around a bit today."

"Sure," Sierra smiled. "Derrick is here today too."

My palms started to sweat again. More people to have to fool. Didn't Anita get that I really didn't need friends? If she noticed my panicked look, she didn't comment on it, giving me an encouraging smile before she walked off to join Ellen back in the indoor. I felt self-conscious as a brief, awkward silence passed between me and Sierra, my pulse speeding up. I'd put on my best pair of jeans and a decent-looking flannel, as well as polished my well-worn paddock boots, but I felt out of place next to Sierra in her fawn-colored breeches, dark green, collared long-sleeved top, and black vest that matched her shiny black tall boots.

"When did you move in over at Heart and Soul?" Sierra asked, grabbing a curry comb and stiff brush before starting to brush out her gelding's sweaty coat.

"A couple of weeks ago," I replied, uncomfortably shifting my weight from one foot to the other. Sierra seemed genuinely friendly, even with Anita gone. Maybe it wasn't all an act just because Anita had been standing here.

"That's cool," Sierra replied. "Are you from around this area?"

I shook my head. "No. I came up from Atlanta."

"I've never been to Georgia. Lived here all my life, and horse farm and vacation don't normally go together. That must have been a heck of a drive." Sierra grabbed a dark green fleece cooler off the metal blanket bar behind her, tossing it up on Wings before doing up the couple of buckles. "Let me put Wings in his stall really quick and then we can go find Derrick."

I stayed where I was, feeling completely out of place in the big barn while Sierra walked her horse to a stall a few feet away. Once she'd turned him loose and latched the door behind her, she hung his halter up and walked back over to me.

"Derrick is probably already in the indoor," she said. "It's about time for Isabel to ride."

I settled for nodding and following along behind her. With Anita having abandoned me, I didn't have much of a choice. We walked out of the barn, passing the flashy black horse, who was now fully tacked. The same guy as before was holding him, roughly yanking on the horse's reins to get him to stand still so his rider could mount up.

"He's a looker, isn't he?" Sierra said, slowing her pace and following my gaze. "Mom and I were honestly kind of surprised when we saw Isabel sign up for the clinic with him. His name is Knight Errant. Isabel showed him on the jumper circuit all summer. Her dad, Rodger, is the head trainer over at River Green Farm and he's super strict about who she is and isn't allowed to ride with. This clinic isn't Rodger's style of training; I was honestly kind of shocked to see her name on the schedule. But Mom is always saying we should be welcoming to anyone who is brave enough to come put themselves on the altar of learning to better communicate with their horses."

I tried to file away every piece of information Sierra was giving me. Anita had already told me a large part of the horse business was about making connections. It was definitely not something I had ever been particularly good at, but I could try. Isabel finally managed to swing up on Knight Errant's back. He tried to bolt but Isabel took a firm hold of the reins, though she looked anything but relaxed.

Sierra resumed her speedy walk and I hurried to catch up with her. When we ducked in through the small door on the side of the indoor, Sierra paused just inside, pursing her lips as she scanned the crowd. It looked like there was a lull between riders right now, Ellen out talking with the clinician while they readjusted a few of the jumps.

"There he is," Sierra said. "Come on; I'll introduce you. Have you met Dr. Thompson yet?"

"No," I answered, though the name sounded slightly familiar, like I'd heard it pop up once or twice over the last few weeks.

"I'm sure you will soon. She's the vet at Still Waters Equine Clinic. We use Still Waters too for vet stuff, like Anita. Derrick is her son and we've gone to school together for like forever at this point. Derrick is at Virginia Tech right now, getting his undergrad in Biology so he can go to vet school, but he likes to come home on the weekends if he can." She dropped her voice as we skirted behind a row of folding chairs. "Also, between you and me, I'm pretty positive he's been in love with Isabel since junior year, but she's been dating Trevor since our sophomore year."

"Is that the guy who was out there at the trailer with her?" I asked. He'd kind of seemed like a jerk, especially with as rough as he'd been with the horse.

"Yeah," Sierra frowned. "He rides with her dad, has for years, and competes on the jumping circuit with Isabel. Honestly, if you ask me, he's an ass. But Isabel seems pretty serious about him."

Note to self, I thought. *Steer clear of Trevor.* Sierra stopped next to a short, dark-haired guy who I assumed was Derrick. He looked up as Sierra took the seat beside him and I took the last empty seat beside her as inconspicuously as possible.

"Hey, Derrick," Sierra said before motioning to me. "This is Meg. She's Anita's new assistant over at Heart and Soul. Meg, Derrick Thompson. Or should I say, soon to be Dr. Derrick Thompson."

Derrick let out a chuckle, shaking his head before shaking my hand. "Not quite doctor anything yet. Got quite a few more years to go. It's nice to meet you, Meg."

"Nice to meet you too," I replied, feeling a little more at ease as Sierra and Derrick switched to discussing Wings and how the gelding had done in the clinic.

I was still leery of getting too close to anyone, but if I had to choose friends, Sierra and Derrick might be alright. They'd been nice enough so far. More than anyone I'd known in Atlanta. *That's because they don't know you're just a big fake—yet.* I bit my lip, trying to ignore the quiver of doubt in my chest. The pounding of hooves at the door to the indoor drew everyone's attention and Isabel entered on Knight Errant, the horse jigging as he walked in and throwing his head against the martingale he wore. He chomped at the bit, not looking any calmer than he had out by the trailers.

The lesson began and Derrick and Sierra fell quiet. Knight Errant was pretty on edge, but even with his skittish behavior, he was a beautiful mover. And if Sierra had been good on a horse, Isabel was flawless. Her position was still practically perfect and her tall build made her look like she was made to sit on a horse. Derrick, I noticed, didn't take his eyes off Isabel even once, lending further proof to Sierra's comment that he had a thing for Isabel.

To my surprise, the clinician had Isabel and Knight Errant stay at the walk for almost the entire lesson. Isabel didn't look like she was bothered by that turn of events, and I honestly couldn't blame her. I wouldn't want to be jumping a horse as hot and spooky as Knight Errant, but Trevor had joined the crowd. He stood by the arena door with a scowl, his arms folded over his chest, and he muttered the occasional curse word under his breath.

"Like I said," Sierra said, keeping her voice low and subtly inclining her head toward him, "an ass."

The lesson continued and by the end of it, Isabel and Knight Errant had progressed to walking over ground poles and doing the tiniest bit of trot work. The horse definitely looked more relaxed at the end of the session than he had at the beginning, which had seemed to be the clinician's whole focus: getting the horse relaxed and Isabel as well so they could be safe and communicate clearly with one another.

I cast a sidelong glance at Trevor again. He still looked pretty pissed. A few weeks ago, I might have found the whole thing kind of ridiculous and boring too, but the more time I spent around Anita, watching her work with the horses at Heart and Soul, along with my lessons with Fuego, I was starting to see that there really was some merit to her slow, methodical approach.

The horses couldn't be in any sort of learning frame of mind if they were afraid and stressed, and we couldn't clearly communicate with them if we didn't learn to harness our patience. What I was learning now wasn't anything like what I had learned at Blue Moon and to be honest, if I was still there, I probably would have never given someone like Anita a second look. The peer pressure of doing things the exact same way everyone else did would have been too great for that. But at Heart and Soul, I felt free to spread my wings and look at things from a different perspective.

After a couple more calm, relaxed trots around the ring during which Knight Errant didn't shoot forward every time he was asked to speed up, the clinician called the session to an end. Isabel had a hesitant smile on her face as she dismounted and began to lead the horse out of the ring, but it vanished as soon as she met Trevor at the arena doorway.

"Damn waste of time and money," Trevor said with a scowl. "I can't believe you made us drive all the way over here for this crap."

Isabel's face crumpled and even Knight Errant seemed to pick up on the tension, throwing his head and tugging at the reins. Derrick's shoulders bunched and one of his hands clenched into a fist as he glowered at Trevor.

"That was a really nice ride, Isabel," Sierra piped up, not even looking Trevor's way. "Thanks for coming; it was great having you."

Isabel bit her lip before giving Sierra a faint half-smile. "Thanks."

"Let's get out of here," Trevor snapped. "I still have two horses to get on today."

He stalked off toward the trailers, Isabel following with Knight Errant, but not before I saw her shoulders droop.

"I can't understand why she even puts up with him," Derrick grumbled.

"They've been together for a while at this point." Sierra shrugged one shoulder. "And I get the vibe she's probably under a lot of pressure with her dad. Sometimes you get so used to things, anything different feels scary."

My chest twinged a little; that was something I could under-stand. Leaving Atlanta and coming here had felt scary—still felt scary, if I were truly honest—but if I'd stayed in Atlanta, there wouldn't have been a future for me. Here, I had a chance, so long as I didn't completely blow it with Anita. But still, taking that first leap had been hard. *And you don't even know if it's actually going to have been worth it,* I thought, squirming slightly in my seat.

Derrick sighed, glumly staring down at his hands. "She just deserved way better than that."

"Yeah, but *she* has to be the one to see that," Sierra replied.

Another horse and rider entered the ring and Sierra turned her attention to the pair, quickly giving me the rundown on who they were, another boarder and client at her family's farm. As Sierra continued to chat while the horse and rider warmed up, I noticed Derrick getting a little more at ease, the tension in his shoulders loosening some, and I found myself relaxing a little more too. Sierra definitely had a way of making the people around her feel more comfortable. I still wasn't entirely sure I wanted to make any friends here. Really, I wasn't sure I could risk having friends without the potential of my whole big lie unraveling, but maybe, just maybe, I could make an exception for the two people sitting next to me. If I were really honest and if I could get over my fear, it would be nice to feel like someone cared.

Chapter Six

SINCE THE CLINIC LAST weekend, Sierra and I had texted a handful of times and I was beginning to think she was pretty damn determined to be my friend, no matter how uncertain I was feeling about the whole friend thing. And even though I was still feeling a little bit like a skittish yearling at the thought of making some real, lasting connections here, it was kind of nice having someone to talk to, especially someone who loved horses as much as I did.

It had been a full month since I'd left Georgia, and Heart and Soul was beginning to feel more like home than Atlanta ever had. Glenda had texted me a whole whooping one time since I'd left, to let me know she was taking me off her AAA membership, and while her lack of caring still kind of hurt, that hurt had been tempered by the fact that by leaving her and everything I'd ever known, I'd managed to find myself closer to the life I'd always dreamed of. Sometimes, I guessed it did take a few seconds of bravery to change your whole life for the better.

And I'm finally starting to get a little more competent around here, I thought, unable to keep a triumphant grin off my face as I tied Winter's rope halter correctly on the first try. Hours of YouTube watching and reading every website I could find on horse care and horse training were paying off. I'd even found the local library last weekend and gotten myself a library card so I could check out every book they had on horses. I'd been reading every chance I got in between chores, training sessions, and lessons.

With the halter securely in place, I clucked to Winter and gently put a feel on the lead line, asking the mare to move forward. She did so willingly and my smile broadened. I was super excited to work with her today. Over the last few weeks, I suspected that Anita had started to notice how much I liked the mare, and she was allowing me to handle Winter's groundwork training session this morning.

I wouldn't be completely on my own, as Anita would be supervising while she long-lined Smoke, but it felt a bit like I'd passed a test of sorts. Anita felt comfortable with me working with one of the greener horses, and that felt good. I was determined not to let her down and show her that I'd been paying close attention to everything she'd taught me these last few weeks.

Leaving the barn behind, I led Winter over to the arena. It was a brisk fall day, the wind blowing the dead leaves off the ground and whipping them up in the air before they floated back down to the browning grass. Winter tensed a little at one of the bigger wind gusts, but at least didn't go into a full-on spook. I took a few deep breaths to try and calm the butterflies that were doing somersaults in my middle. Today was going to be an easy day. The instructions Anita had given me were for some basic forequarter and hindquarter yields on the line and then I would switch Winter into the leather training cavesson and we'd do some some simple stretching work over poles to help her release her topline and find better alignment in her spine. I'd done the exercises with Fuego enough times that I felt pretty proficient. I could do them with Winter too, even if she didn't have the experience that Fuego did.

When we reached the arena gate, Anita already had Smoke on the long lines. The lanky light grey horse walked around in various-sized circles and straight lines while Anita held on to the two very long leads that allowed her to be both farther behind and farther away from him. Long lining wasn't something I'd ever seen done prior to coming to Heart and Soul but it looked pretty cool—albeit a bit complicated. I hoped I'd get to try it for myself someday.

I led Winter through the gate and grabbed a couple of plastic orange cones, setting them up in a corner of the ring where we would hopefully stay out of Anita and Smoke's way. Anita smiled and called a greeting before asking Smoke to move from a walk into a trot.

Once the cones were set up, I started working on Winter's forequarter and hindquarter yields. At first, things were going well. The mare was softening up as she started responding to my lighter cues, but then a gust of wind blew over one of the cones and caused her to spook. Winter jumped sideways, pulling hard on the line and almost jerking it out of my hands. My heart leapt but I managed to bring her hindquarters back around and keep her from running off. She stood stock still, her nostrils fluttering as she loudly snorted, her neck rigid as she warily eyed the fallen cone. My heart was pounding so strongly, I could feel it in my neck. I was sure that Anita had seen my mistake and my shoulders tensed as I waited for the scolding that would be sure to follow.

"Just give her a minute and help her get calm again," Anita called. "This wind is going to have everyone a little more up and on alert today."

I glanced over at Anita and Smoke, the latter of whom didn't seem at all bothered by the wind. Granted he *was* a lot older than Winter and he'd been in training with Anita a lot longer. Taking another deep breath, I squared my shoulders. I could do this. I focused on getting Winter connected with me again with a few more hindquarter yields, along with asking her to lower her head and release some of the tension in her neck. A few minutes later, she seemed much less concerned about the fallen cone and gusty wind. I couldn't help but smile as I led the mare over to the fence. I was actually starting to get the hang of all of this. I was one step closer to making a dream of a life with horses a reality.

After exchanging her rope halter for the leather cavesson and lead that hung on a fence post, we resumed our work. The cavesson exercises were newer to me, but Winter was responding well, lengthening her neck and her stride as she became more relaxed in her body. But then the wind picked up again and Winter tensed, whipping her head toward the tree line at the back of the arena.

I hesitated. We'd done all the exercises at the walk and that had been going fine; well, up until a few seconds ago. I'd read Anita's training plan for the mare three times this morning and I knew a touch of trot work was part of today's planned routine. She hadn't spooked super badly yet and Anita was watching. I needed to at least try and make it happen. I was the one responsible for making sure Winter practiced the appropriate exercises today, after all. But that, it turned out, was absolutely the wrong move.

The second I asked for the trot, Winter's head shot up and she only made it two strides before half barging into me and bolting.

For a split second, I tried to hold on, but Winter ripped the lead right out of my hand, leaving behind a burning, stinging pain. I winced, my face flushing with heat as the mare took off down to the other end of the arena where Anita was working with Smoke. *Great,* I thought, my stomach dropping. *Way to completely blow it the first time you get a little extra responsibility.*

"Sorry," I called, walking as quickly as I could, my shoulders hunched. I knew better than to run around the horses, but it also wasn't exactly safe to have Winter tearing around the ring. Anita brought Smoke to a halt, safely securing the long lines. Winter had finally stopped her mad dash and was grazing on the little bits of grass at the edge of the arena, a few feet away from Smoke.

"I'm really sorry," I said when I reached Anita and the mare, not able to meet Anita's gaze.

"You alright?" Anita asked.

"Yeah," I said with a tight nod.

She handed me back Winter's lead, but when I went to take it, the sharp stinging pain in my hand returned and I hissed.

"Let me see," Anita said, gesturing to my hand.

I held it out to her, trying to not to cringe. A serious scolding had to be coming at any moment. I just knew it. I only hoped my big screw-up didn't cost me my job.

"Ah," Anita said, surprising me with the faintest of wry grins. "A little learn burn, I see."

"I didn't mean to let go of her when she spooked. I tried to hold onto her."

"I'm glad you did let go. I'd rather you do that than get dragged. We're in a fully fenced arena; it's not like she was going to be able to take off down the driveway toward the road. Accidents happen and we all make bad judgement calls. My question for you is, what could you have done differently that you're going to do next time?"

I blinked rapidly. That meant there *was* going to be a next time, right?

"I… I guess maybe I shouldn't have asked her to go into the trot when I did. She wasn't really relaxed and ready. Next time, I guess the thing to do would be to make sure she's really calm and ready at the walk before asking for the trot."

"Good," Anita replied. "I write the training plans every week, but they are absolutely *always* open to change. We have to be present with the horses and where they're at on any given day, and that means being willing to change plans. In Winter's case, a change of plans likely would have been the better choice for today. No good comes from rushing a horse who isn't ready just because it's on the training plan." She paused, her expression softening a bit. "You're going to make mistakes in this business. The important part is that you learn from them."

I nodded, my thoughts still reeling. This had definitely not been what I'd been expecting. At Blue Moon, any time I messed up, I was guaranteed to be in for a long lecture that probably involved some curse words thrown in and one or two remarks about me being an idiot. Hell, Glenda had been spewing those things at me too every time I did something wrong from the moment I'd stepped through her front door.

"I'm… not in trouble?" I asked, furrowing my brow.

"I don't punish horses and I don't punish people," Anita said, handing me the lead. "In my experience, it doesn't do much good, and you've clearly learned your lesson. I think the wisest thing for you and Winter to do would be to go back over to where you were in the ring and take a few moments to connect with your breath. Ask her to lower her head a few times, help her feel good and relaxed again, and then practice an exercise she's confident with before calling it a day. The rest of the exercises can be revisited again tomorrow, with a new, fresh slate. And once you're done with Winter, make sure you go in and clean that burn on your hand off good and hit it with some triple antibiotic. Keep it covered, keep it clean, and keep applying the ointment for a few days and you should be good to go. There's a first aid kit in the bathroom in the apartment, under the sink."

I thanked her, taking the leather lead with my good hand as the tension in my shoulders released. I had messed up today, but it sounded like Anita was going to give me another chance. Winter blew out a loud breath, giving her neck a light shake and we walked back over to the corner of the arena with the cones. As Anita resumed working with Smoke, I took a few moments to just stand with Winter and focus on my breathing in an effort to calm my own self again. The mare would be reading my every move and emotion; I needed to be calm and centered myself if I wanted her to be. Once I had gotten Winter to lower her head a few times, her body language shifting from worried to relaxed, I asked her to back up between two of the cones, and then we left the arena behind to head back to the barn.

Once in the barn aisle, I walked Winter over to a tie ring to brush her down before turning her back out. As I went over her dappled grey coat with a stiff brush, a niggle of guilt made my throat tighten ever so slightly. I didn't like lying to Anita. She was a good person and she didn't deserve it. No one had ever been so patient with me before; I was honestly starting to wonder if the woman was some sort of saint. But I also didn't want to find myself out of a job. More than that, I didn't want to leave the ranch. I had grown to love it here and I wanted to stay. Was it possible that if I told Anita how much I'd embellished my resume and how little I did actually know, she'd be willing to listen and not immediately kick me out? I bit my lip so hard it hurt, fumbling some with the brush. The risk felt way too big and quite frankly, I didn't know if I had the guts to come face to face with the consequences of the truth.

Chapter Seven

One week after the incident where Winter had gotten away from me in the arena, I was staring down my biggest challenge yet. Anita had gone out of town with her sister, Elena, for a minivacation. It was the first vacation that Anita had apparently taken in years, and I would be holding down things at the ranch until she got back. True, she wasn't going far, just up to D.C., but I was feeling pretty pleased that she'd trusted me with such a big responsibility. A little guilt still gnawed at me over not being one hundred percent honest to Anita, but I'd been doing everything I could to learn as much as I could and from the looks of things, it was paying off. Maybe, just maybe, I could get away with never having to reveal the truth.

Anita had left early yesterday morning and so far, I'd had a pretty relaxing two days. The weather was nice, which meant the horses had stayed out most of the night last night and made morning chores easy, and yesterday, with the beautiful weather, I'd had a good groundwork session and ride with Fuego. I appreciated that Anita had given me permission to work with him some while she was away. Not only did I enjoy my time with the good-natured older gelding, it was good practice to keep improving my skills. Over the last week, I'd gotten to work with Winter again and with one of the training horses, Storm Heart, under Anita's watchful eye. That, combined with Anita trusting me to watch the ranch in her absence, felt like progress.

My little Honda sputtered a little as I pulled into the parking lot of the local tack store, The Grey Fox Tack & Feed. I frowned as I found a place to park. I probably needed to get that noise looked at. I'd have to ask Anita if she knew a good mechanic. Thank goodness I'd been getting a decent-sized paycheck the last few weeks. Rolling out of the car, I headed for the front of the shop, trying not to be too self-conscious with my beat-up car and cracked paddock boots. The boots were the big reason I was here. After buying groceries this week, I'd had a little bit money left over and Anita had mentioned last week that the Grey Fox offered consignment. I was hoping I could find a lightly-used pair of boots in my size. I sure as hell couldn't afford a new pair, even with my increase in income. Boots were expensive.

As I stepped into the tack shop, the bell on the door gave a slight jingle. I tried not to feel too self-conscious about my well-worn jeans and the sorry state of my boots. The shop smelled strongly of leather and all around me were sparkling new saddles, bridles, halters, and riding outfits. It was basically horse girl heaven. A twangy country song played softly throughout the store and the older woman behind the desk welcomed me to the shop.

"Could you point me to the consignment section?" I asked her.

"Sure thing," she answered. "You want to head to the back of the store. There's a separate room just for consignment."

"Thanks," I replied.

Shoving my hands in the back pockets of my jeans, I walked off in the direction she'd pointed. There was a little twinge in my chest as I glanced around at the beautiful sets of matching saddle pads and leg wraps, accented by gleaming rhinestone bridles. The woman at the front had been nice, but I was pretty sure it had been obvious I wasn't her usual clientele. I'd learned pretty quickly at Blue Moon that, like it or not, money mattered to a large part of the horse world. Most of the girls who'd ridden there had come from money and I had always been left feeling like I never quite fit in. It was yet another reason I wanted so badly to stay at Heart and Soul. Anita was obviously pretty well off, but the ranch was about the horses. It wasn't there to flaunt anyone's wealth or ego and she'd never made me feel bad for my worn clothes, beat-up boots, or lack of designer helmet.

The shop wasn't very busy. I only saw one person browsing riding helmets, and eventually, I found the consignment room. After a little searching, I found a couple pairs of paddock boots, which all looked to be in pretty good shape. I started checking the sizing and pricing, and as luck would have it, the third pair I picked up fit both my budget and my shoe size. I slipped out of my worn boots and tried the new ones one, pleased when they fit well. I'd just picked them up and tucked them under my elbow when I heard someone call my name. Turning around, I saw Sierra walking over with Derrick right behind her. Sierra had texted me earlier this week saying that Derrick would be coming for fall break and that the three of us should hang out. I'd been putting her off, but their friendly smiles were enough to make me reconsider.

I did really like Sierra and Derrick. Maybe I could be brave and try to make some real friends here.

"Hey," I said when they reached me.

"Hey, how are you?" Sierra asked with a smile. "Mom said you're at Heart and Soul by yourself while Anita is up in D.C. If you need anything, don't hesitate to call."

"Thanks," I replied. Anita had given me Ellen's number and told me I could call the MacFarlanes for anything, but I was still determined to manage on my own and prove to Anita that I was as capable of this job as she thought I was. Still, the offer was nice. "Everything's been okay so far."

"I love checking this room," Sierra said, wandering over to a nearby pile of saddle pads. "Mom sent me because we need a new pair of stirrup leathers for one of the lesson saddles, but I can't stop myself from looking at all the consignment items every time I come in. Horse life and budgets, am I right?"

I gave a light laugh, having a hard time wiping the smile off my face. I really did like Sierra. I'd gleaned that Haven Hills had been in her family for a couple of generations and in their case, the farm was very much a working farm. They made enough to get by and keep things going, but they weren't rolling in cash by any means.

"And Derrick just came along because he wanted to get out of dealing with a constipated pig," Sierra said.

Derrick shoved his hands in his front pockets, ducking his chin a bit sheepishly. "I'm going to school to specialize in equine veterinary medicine, remember? Not large animal." He paused, glancing over at me. "My mom does both, which, yeah… sometimes means constipated pigs."

Sierra laughed and I couldn't stop myself from joining in, especially with the smile on Derrick's face.

"Sierra, is that you?"

Another woman pushed into the consignment area. She looked to be around Anita's age, in her early to mid-forties. Rhinestones shaped like small flowers shined on her peach button up plaid shirt and her dark wash jeans and turquoise and tan cowboy boots were spotless. Her blond hair was twisted up in a bun with not a single hair out of place. Sierra turned away from the saddle pads, her smile suddenly looking strained, and even Derrick seemed to be eying the newcomer with a hint of suspicion.

"Hi, Willa," Sierra said.

"Did your mother ever get that clinic of yours filled?" Willa asked, bringing a hand to her chest. "You know, I felt so bad telling her that Wyatt and I couldn't send any of our clients there, not in good conscience. We just had so many questions for the clinician; you know, whether they truly *were* using natural principles and were up to date on the latest research. We've put so much effort into building our brand, you know. Our clients have such exceedingly high expectations of us. The pressure truly is so much greater than most people even know."

"The clinic filled fine," Sierra replied, her jaw tightening ever so slightly.

"Oh, wonderful," Willa replied. "I'm so happy to hear. Wyatt is doing a clinic in two weeks, you know. And I'll be doing the behavior portion. Please do tell your mother that we would love to have any riders from Haven Hills join us. Oh, I suppose perhaps mention to the riders that we do have one training spot open. Very exclusive, you know. Wyatt and I don't take just anyone."

"I will," Sierra said, tapping her fingers on the side of her leg.

Willa turned her attention to me, a slight frown marring her face. "Oh, who is your little friend, Sierra? I don't think I've seen her before."

"Meg," I piped up, even if my stomach was quivering. There was something about Willa that felt intimidating. As if she were silently judging me while pretending to be welcoming and interested. "Meg Beckett. I just started working at Heart and Soul Ranch a few weeks ago."

"Ah, yes, Anita Lancaster's place." Willa wrinkled her nose a touch, fishing something out of her pocket before handing me a shiny business card. "Well, if at some point you decide you want to learn about real natural and holistic horse care, here's my card. Wyatt and I are always looking for qualified help."

I took the card; I really didn't know what else to do without making the whole situation even more awkward than it already was. But had this woman seriously just met me, subtly insulted my boss, and then wanted me to come work for her?

"So nice seeing all of you," Willa said. "I'm afraid I have to get running. Don't forget to tell your mother about the clinic, Sierra."

I stared at Willa's retreating back, slightly dumbfounded. The metallic foil on the edges of the business card I still held glinted in the fluorescent shop lighting. The silhouette of a horse grazing under a tree was dead center, with Willa's name and contact information in a bold Serif font. There were a surprising number of letters after her name, not that I knew what they all meant.

"Well," Sierra said with a grimace as soon as Willa was out of earshot. "You have now met Willa Evans. Part one of the business partner duo that run Nature's Grove Farm."

"I…wow." I glanced down at the card again, reading the text that listed Willa as a horse trainer, behaviorist, saddle fitter, massage therapist, some other kind of bodywork therapist I'd never heard of before, and nutritionist. "Is she always like that?"

"Basically, yeah," Derrick replied. "I mean, she's pretty smart. She toes the line with her health services just enough to keep my mom or any of the other local vets from reporting her to the state, but yeah. That's Willa."

"And she's actually all of these things?" I waved the card.

"That's the pitch." Sierra shrugged. "I'm really not trying to badmouth a neighbor, but some things in the horse industry are a lot of smoke and mirrors. And that's not limited to the world of show horses and sport horses."

I nodded, shoving the business card in my back pocket, not that I ever planned on calling the number on it. If I'd learned nothing else over the last few weeks, it was that while Anita might be unconventional, she wasn't smoke and mirrors. She was the real deal and for her, the most important thing was helping the horses.

"Anyway," Sierra said, turning back to the saddle pads and picking up a rich forest green one with a pretty gold trim before checking the price tag. "In Wings' colors and just eight bucks. Definitely in my price range."

I felt a little less self-conscious with my used boots as we made our way back to the checkout counter. Maybe I would be able to fit in around here after all, people like Willa Evans aside. I checked out after Sierra and then the three of us made our way out to the parking lot, shopping bags in hand.

"Seriously, if you need anything, give us a call," Sierra said when we reached my Honda. "We're only like twenty minutes away. I know when Mom and Dad have gone out of town and it's just me watching the farm, I swear, it's like the horses plan that something is going to happen."

"Thanks," I replied, unlocking the driver's side door. "Hopefully everything stays quiet, but I'll keep that in mind."

"I hope so too. See you later."

I slipped into the driver's seat, waving at Sierra and Derrick as they walked back over to a muddy dark blue truck that bore the Haven Hills logo. Tossing my boots in the passenger seat, I turned the key in the ignition and got on my way back to Heart and Soul. The drive from the Grey Fox wasn't too terribly long and I enjoyed the scenery and peacefulness of the backcountry roads. As I passed a rolling hay field, part of me still couldn't believe I was here. This was my dream and Culpeper was starting to feel like home. When I rolled down the ranch's driveway, the Honda sputtered a little again and I patted the wheel.

"Just give me another week, baby," I murmured, "and then I promise I'll get you to a mechanic."

Once I'd parked, I got out and carried my boots up to the apartment. A glance at my phone told me it was about time for afternoon feed-up and after slipping on my new boots, I jogged back down the stairs to the barn. My feet were so much more comfortable in the new boots and I had a smile on my face as I headed over to the run-ins to start grabbing halters and bringing horses in. These next few days were going to go great.

My smile and blooming confidence, however, were short-lived. The first set of horses was out in their paddock, but when I walked over to halter Winter, I froze at the sight of red streaks on the mare's dappled grey neck. I hurried over to the mare, my heart hammering. Winter swung her head around to look at me, seemingly unstressed despite the ragged gashes and the streaks of dried blood.

"What in the hell did you do, pretty girl?" I said, fumbling with the halter as I slid it over her face.

As I buckled it in place, my gaze fell on the fence a few feet away from us. The middle board was broken, the now sharp edges sticking up toward the sky.

"Ah," I said, not feeling that much better after my discovery. "So that's the culprit. Let's go see what you did."

Thankfully, Winter followed along beside me without issue and we walked over to the fence. The board was definitely split and little flecks of blood told me the broken wood had probably done the damage to the mare's neck. There were little bits of green grass on the other side of the fence and with the way the grass in the paddock had mostly died, I suspected Winter had most likely been trying to get herself a little treat.

"You had hay, you know," I said with a sigh. "Come on, then. Let's get you cleaned up."

I didn't know a whole lot about equine first aid, but I'd been reading up on it and after taking a better look at Winter's neck back in the barn, I thought I could manage this on my own. The cuts didn't look all that bad. I'd clean them off and then put some ointment on them. Simple enough, right? The fence would be the harder fix, but I knew where the power drill was, along with the extra fence boards Anita kept on hand. I could make it work.

Leading Winter into the wash stall, I tied her and set to cleaning her wounds off with a clean rag and some water. As I worked, it niggled at me that I could call Sierra, but I shied away from it. I wanted to prove to Anita that she hadn't made a mistake in hiring me, that I could take care of things on my own. This wasn't that bad. Not really.

After putting a wound ointment on Winter's neck, I put her into her stall for dinner and made the decision to bring the rest of the horses in, get them eating, and then tackle the fence. To my relief, the horses seemed to know that time was of the essence. Once I'd brought them all into their stalls and thrown feed, I gathered up the power drill, screws, and a fence board before returning to the paddock.

I still had a half hour or so before the sun fully set for the night, and that turned out to be a very good thing. Who knew a power drill could be so tricky to use? I let out more than my fair share of curses as I fought to line up the board, hold it there, and not strip the screw. Eventually, I had to resort to flipping through YouTube videos until I finally got the technique sort of down. Thank you, technology.

By the time I trudged back into the barn with the broken board and tools, I was tired, sore, and ready for a shower, food, and bed. I stashed the broken board back in a corner of the hay room and took the two lone broken screws I'd found in the grass back to the feed room to safely discard in the trash can. I was relieved I'd found them; if one of the horses had stepped on them, they could have seriously injured themselves. Despite the scrapes on her neck, Winter had eaten all her dinner and was eager to go back out with her herd. That, I was happy to see. Hopefully her injuries would heal up in a few days and she'd be as good as new.

"No more breaking fence boards, okay," I told her as I led her back into the run-in. "I even put a little extra hay in the hay nets for you guys."

After I removed her halter, the mare wandered off with the other horses, back out into the paddock. Hopefully all the horses would make good choices tonight and I wouldn't have any more surprises in the morning. Once chores were done, I went back upstairs to the apartment. I had just enough time to fix some dinner before I had to go back down for night check. As I was rummaging through the fridge, trying to decide on dinner, I got a text from Sierra, asking how things were going. I hesitated, unsure if I should tell her about Winter or not. Finally, I settled on telling her everything was fine for now. *I've got this,* I told myself as I pulled out a container of leftover mac and cheese. I was determined to make sure Anita didn't regret leaving me in charge, and that meant handling anything unexpected that the horses or the farm threw at me. I *had* to do this on my own. I couldn't afford to lose this new life I'd come to love.

Chapter Eight

By the next day, I'd hoped that Winter's wounds would be showing signs of healing, but that was definitely not the case. Anita was due home tomorrow and quite frankly, I was starting to panic. As I stared at Winter in the wash stall, the fluorescent light above me quietly humming, I worried my lower lip, the bundle of knotted-up nerves that had taken up residence in my middle making me feel slightly nauseous.

The scrapes on Winter's neck did *not* look better. In fact, they looked worse, with two of them having become more and more swollen over the course of the day. If I touched the swollen area, Winter would flinch and move away as if the spots were painful. My stomach churned the longer I stared at the ugly-looking swelling. I thought I had done everything right, but it turned out I was just as incompetent as I'd feared.

I pulled my phone out of the back pocket of my jeans, running my thumb along the edge of the dark blue hard plastic case. Anita had told me she'd had me authorized to call Still Water Equine Clinic for any veterinary services while she was out of town. I'd hoped I wouldn't have to do that, but Winter was clearly uncomfortable and I didn't know what to do to help her. I had to make the call.

With it being a Sunday evening, it was outside of normal business hours, which would mean an expensive emergency call. Hopefully when Anita got the bill, she would understand. Swallowing hard, I pulled up Still Waters' number in my phone. I'd make the call, have the vet out, and then give a report on the situation to Anita. Hopefully I hadn't screwed up so badly that I'd caused Winter to end up with some sort of serious injury. If that were the case, not only would I likely be kissing my job goodbye, I would feel even worse than I did right now for hurting the mare I'd grown to love. I paced the aisleway in front of the wash stall as the phone rang, silently pleading for Dr. Thompson to answer.

"Still Waters Equine. This is Dr. Thompson."

"Hi, Dr. Thompson," I said, clearing my throat, my nerves making my palms sweat. "This is Meg Beckett, at Heart and Soul Ranch."

"Hey, Meg, what can I do for you?"

"I, uh, one of the mares here has some bad cuts on her neck that I think you need to look at. I'm worried it can't wait until Anita gets back tomorrow."

"Of course. I can be over your way in about thirty minutes. Can you tell me what happened to her neck?"

As I tried to reel in my growing anxiety and calm my racing heart in order to form a coherent sentence, I appreciated Dr. Thompson's kind, patient tone. "She tangled with a fence yesterday. I think she was trying to get to the grass on the other side and broke the fence rail. I thought the cuts would clear up in a day or two, but it looks like things are only getting worse."

"We'll get her all fixed. I'm on my way and will see you shortly."

"Thank you so much," I told her before hanging up.

Shoving my phone back in my pocket, I walked back over to Winter.

"I promise I'm going to get you taken care of, sweet girl," I said, petting her shoulder. "I'm sorry I don't know what in the hell I'm doing."

The mare flicked her ears back, listening to my voice, before letting out a low breath. The thirty minutes waiting for Dr. Thompson felt like an eternity. I fretted over what was wrong with Winter, about how this time tomorrow I likely wouldn't even have this job anymore, and where in the hell I was going to go next. I was so very far away from everything I'd ever known and getting fired wasn't going to be a good look when I was forced to go job hunting.

The rumbling of a diesel engine echoed into the barn and Winter pricked her ears, my pulse kicking up another notch. *That means the vet is here,* I told myself, fiddling with my phone again as I listened to the slam of a truck door. *Which means Winter will get taken care of.*

I peered out of the little window at the back of the wash stall. The sun had set, which meant it was too dark to see much, but the floodlights outside the barn allowed me to make out a little bit of the parking lot. Dr. Thompson was pulling things out of the different compartments built into her truck, though it was still too dark to tell what all she was grabbing. A few moments later, she headed for the barn.

"Thank you so much for coming," I told her, meeting her in the aisleway before the two of us walked to the wash stall. "I wasn't sure if I should call or not, but she seems really uncomfortable."

"If in doubt, it's always better to call," Dr. Thompson said, setting down a metal pail and what looked like a plastic grooming tote that had been turned into a caddy of medical supplies. "Always better to catch things sooner rather than later."

Dr. Thompson stepped into the wash stall with Winter and began to inspect the mare's neck.

"Got yourself into a tangle with a fence, did you, pretty girl?" Dr. Thompson said, her tone gentle as she began to probe the swollen spots.

Winter pinned back her ears and wrinkled her nostrils, flinching away from the vet's touch.

"She broke a fence rail, right?" Dr. Thompson asked.

"Yeah," I answered.

"Have you given any Bute or done any cold-hosing?"

My chest constricted. Thanks to my reading, I knew that Bute was a pain-killer, but what in the heck was cold-hosing?

"Umm... no, I haven't," I said. "I did clean the cuts with soap and water and then applied an ointment Anita keeps in the first aid kit, but it just seems to be getting worse."

"The trouble we can have with broken fence rails is they can get a splinter—or more than one sometimes. Especially if any of these were punctures. Things can get down in there and cause trouble."

A niggle of guilt made my stomach feel rock hard. Listening to the vet talk felt like more proof that I didn't have nearly the experience I needed for this job.

Dr. Thompson returned to her caddy, rummaging around before pulling out a large pair of hair clippers; sort of like what you'd see in a hair salon, but way bigger. "Do you know how she is with clippers? I can always sedate her if need be, but I want to remove a little bit of the hair to get a better look."

"I think she's okay?" I replied. "I've never clipped her or seen her clipped, but I don't remember Anita mentioning it being an issue."

"We'll start small and see how she does."

I helped Dr. Thompson find an outlet to plug in her clippers and to my relief, Winter didn't seem at all bothered by them. I stood at the mare's head to help keep her still, but she only pulled away a little as Dr. Thompson buzzed off the hair around the wounds. Once Dr. Thompson was done giving Winter an awkward little buzz cut, she pulled on a pair of surgical gloves and put on a tiny little headlamp with a super bright light.

"This next part might get bloody," she said. "You might want to look away if you're squeamish."

I contemplated insisting that I was fine, but prior to Winter's incident, I hadn't really seen blood on a horse. That had only been a little bit of blood and it had still been enough to make me feel kind of queasy. In the end, I decided to save face, angling myself away from Dr. Thompson as she went to work.

"Ah, here are our little culprits," she said a few moments later. "Definitely a few splinters in here."

I waited a few moments more before Dr. Thompson gave the all clear. When I turned back around, there was still a little bit of blood, but she'd cleaned most of it up. Laying on a bundle of gauze near the pail were three splinters of wood; two small and one large.

"I can't believe I missed those," I said, my face flushing with embarrassment. How in the hell had I not seen those?

"Like I said, it happens." Dr. Thompson took off her gloves, turning them inside out before discarding them. "Splinters aren't always easy to find on these guys, especially in deeper wounds. Now, one of the best things you can do to help her heal is flush and cold-hose these wounds daily. But you want to make sure you use gentle water pressure; you don't want anything harsh. I want you to flush these areas at least twice a day and then three to four times a day, I just want you to run cold water over the injured area of her neck to help bring the swelling down. I'm going to go ahead and prescribe her some Bute for a couple of days to help with the pain and swelling, as well as a short course of antibiotics since we had foreign bodies in the wounds. Just to make sure she doesn't develop an infection."

I nodded, my thoughts whirling. "Is… is it okay if I write this all down?"

"Absolutely."

I excused myself and walked off into the tack room, grabbing a pen and a piece of paper from the training journals Anita kept in the small cupboard. When I returned to the wash stall, Dr. Thompson gave me my very long list of instructions. It honestly felt like it would be a lot to juggle on top of regular chores, but Anita would be back tomorrow and I would do whatever I needed to do to make sure Winter was okay. I couldn't help but feel that it was my fault—my own ignorance, really—that the mare was in pain right now.

After leaving me with a bottle of antibiotics and a tube of Bute, Dr. Thompson headed out, apparently off to another call to treat a colicking horse at another farm. I got Winter settled back out with her herd and then headed back up to the apartment, absolutely dreading what was coming next. It was a little late, just after ten, and I didn't want to bother Anita, but I needed to let her know what had happened and that I'd had to call the vet. Closing the apartment door behind me, I went and sank down onto the couch, pulling up Anita's number and wishing I could get rid of the uncomfortable, jittery feeling in my middle. I hit the *send call* button and for a minute, I thought it would go to voice mail, but then Anita answered.

"Hello?" she said, her voice a little groggy.

"Hey, Anita, it's Meg."

"Hey, Meg. Is everything okay?" she asked, immediately more alert.

"Um, yeah," I replied, fidgeting with the zipper of my jacket. "Well, I mean, it is now. Winter broke a fence rail on Friday. I fixed the fence and cleaned up her wound, but it wasn't getting better so I called Dr. Thompson tonight and she came and pulled a few splinters out of Winter's neck."

"I'm glad you called her and got it taken care of before it turned into something more serious," Anita said with a slight sigh of what I hoped was relief. "I'll be back tomorrow to help you tackle any wound care. I'm dropping Elena off at home before heading to the ranch, but I should actually be back a little early, closer to noon."

"Sounds great," I said, my shoulders tensing as I braced myself for the yelling that was sure to follow. Only, it didn't come.

Was that seriously it? I mean, she'd gone out of town and one of the horses had gotten hurt on my watch. If anything like this had happened at Blue Moon, Janet would have been livid. Hell, if I'd done something as simple as forget to move the clothes from the washer to the dryer, Glenda would lose it.

"Let me know if anything else comes up," Anita said. "And if you need anything, don't forget you can call the MacFarlanes."

"Will do," I said before we hung up.

I dropped my phone in my lap, putting my face in my hands with a sigh. Anita didn't *seem* that upset, but who knew; maybe she was waiting to chew me out in person. I barely stifled a groan as I thought over the events of the last two days. I probably should have called the MacFarlanes on Friday instead of lying to Sierra and telling her everything was fine. I didn't know anything about taking care of sick horses, other than what I'd read online and in books, but my damn pride had gotten in the way.

Checking the time on my phone, I noticed that it was inching closer to eleven. I needed to get a shower and get to bed. I had a long day tomorrow, which was going to include figuring out how to give medicine to a horse. Dr. Thompson had given me some pointers, but it was going to be trial by fire until Anita got home. *And tomorrow I have to tell Anita the truth,* I thought, my chest clenching again. *I should have been honest with her from the start.* I rubbed my aching chest and then got up from the couch, heading for the bathroom. I couldn't keep lying like this. This weekend could have turned out so much worse than it had. If one of the horses ever got seriously hurt because of me not telling the truth and not knowing what I was doing, I didn't think I'd be able to live with myself. All I could hope was that by some small miracle, come tomorrow, I'd still have a job and a roof over my head.

Chapter Nine

By noon the following day, I was a nervous wreck. And not only was I a nervous wreck, I was a nervous wreck who was splattered in chalky white paste from the antibiotics that Dr. Thompson had left for Winter. She'd told me my best bet was soaking them, since most horses weren't going to eat the large pills whole, then putting them in a syringe to give to Winter.

It had sounded easy enough and the first part had been a breeze. The pills had puffed up into a sticky paste, just like Dr. Thompson had said they would, but then everything had gone downhill. Getting the mixture into the syringe without spilling it all was not easy, and that hadn't even been the most difficult part. No, the most challenging part of the whole fiasco had been trying to get Winter to take her medicine. For as mild mannered as she'd been last night, she'd wanted no part in taking the antibiotics. In the end, I was pretty sure I'd gotten more of them on me than I'd actually gotten in her mouth.

I closed the run door and latched it, heaving a heavy sigh as I looked down at my white-splattered jacket. I sure as heck hoped this came out in the wash. As soon as I'd turned her loose, Winter had ditched me to go back out with her herd mates. I hung her halter back up on the hooks outside the run-in and moments later, my pulse quickened at the tell-tale rumble of a truck pulling into the parking lot. I looked at my clothes again with a grimace. I'd hoped to clean up before Anita got home. So much for that.

Squaring my shoulders, I walked down the barn aisle, even if everything in me wanted to run back upstairs. I had to get this over with and come clean. If this weekend had made nothing else clear to me, it was that lying about my experience might very well put a horse at risk. I'd been lucky what had happened with Winter hadn't been worse. What if I hadn't called Dr. Thompson and the mare had gotten an infection? Anita deserved the truth, but more than that, the horses deserved someone who knew how to take care of them. And that someone was most definitely not me.

Anita met me at the barn doors and I could feel my face flush. I dropped my gaze, staring hard at my boots, which were also covered in flecks of thick white paste. I looked like a walking disaster. I mean, that's basically what I was at this point, wasn't it?

"Ah," Anita said. "The joys of administering SMZs."

I risked glancing up at her, the lightness in her tone surprising me. "Yeah, it… ah, it didn't go well."

"I haven't gotten to work with Winter much on things like oral meds yet. But sometimes things happen and we have to move things like that to the forefront. I'll show you the best way to do her meds today, but it's likely going to take some time before she feels comfortable and confident with what we're doing."

I nodded, my throat tight and my mouth dry. I wondered if there was even going to be a next time. *You have to say something,* I told myself. *Think of Winter.*

"I need to talk with you," I said, my heart pounding in my ears.

Anita's brow wrinkled and she slightly tilted her head. "Alright. Why don't you get cleaned up and come up to the house. That'll give me a bit of time to get my things in and start unpacking."

I swallowed hard. Things were going from bad to worse. Anita had never invited me up to the house before. Did she already know how much of a screwup I was? Was she going to fire me there? Somehow, I managed a nod and she returned to her truck while I clambered back up the stairs, my legs feeling like lead weights.

Thankfully I had a clean set of clothes to change into and I used a washcloth to wipe the bits of antibiotic paste off my face, neck, and hands. When I went to brush my hair, I noticed a little bit of the sticky paste caked into a few strands. I grumbled under my breath as I worked to brush it out. I didn't have time to shower right now, but I sure as hell was getting a good thorough shower tonight.

Trying not to dwell on the possibility that tonight might be my last warm shower for a while, if Anita even let me stay that long, I jogged back down the stairs and headed back up to the house. As I walked up the gravel path that led up the hill to the little brick ranch Anita called home, my gaze strayed to the distant woods. The trees were bathed in brilliant tones of gold and red, and the beautiful Blue Ridge mountains loomed larger than life behind them. Moisture pricked my eyes and I blinked it back. I'd only been here a little over a month and I'd miss this beautiful place so damn much.

Once I reached the house, Anita let me inside and led the way into the kitchen. At her instruction, I settled down at a chair at the table, rubbing my thumbs together in my lap. Anita looked as calm as ever as she walked over to an electric tea kettle.

"Would you like some tea?" she asked. "I know it's brisk out there today."

It had been a little chilly and I was tempted by the offer of a warm drink, but my stomach was churning so badly, I declined. Anita made herself a drink, the pungent herbal scent mixing with the sweet smell of honey, before she came to sit across from me at the table.

"So," she said, "you had something you needed to tell me?"

My palms were sweating, my face and the back of my neck growing hot. How did I say this? How did I tell her I was just a liar? Finally, I settled for blurting it out.

"I lied," I said, not able to meet her gaze, focusing on the smooth grain of the wood table instead. "About everything. I… I don't really have any experience with horses. Well, I mean, I do have some experience, but not as much as I said on my resume and in the interview."

"I see." Anita made a humming noise before taking a sip of her tea.

"I didn't mean to lie." I didn't quite know why I was plunging on. There was no way to dig myself out of this mess, but Anita wasn't stopping me. Not yet, at least. "I just… I lived with my aunt, in Atlanta, after my parents died. There wasn't any money for me to go to college or anything and she said I was eighteen and not her responsibility anymore. So she was kicking me out at the end of the summer. And I needed a job, and a place to stay. And I love horses; I've always loved horses. I did work at a barn in Atlanta, but I just cleaned the stalls and every once in a while, I would get a riding lesson. But I found your help wanted post online and I thought if I read enough and studied hard enough, I could make it work. This is what I've always wanted to do, but…"

A lump in my throat made me stop and I swallowed against it before continuing. "But the fact that I'm an idiot who doesn't know anything almost got Winter seriously hurt. Someone else would have known what a puncture wound was and how to take care of it. And I didn't." I paused, blinking back the tears that stung my eyes in earnest now. "I understand if you decide to fire me."

Anita studied me for a long moment, sipping her tea again, and I shifted in my seat under her scrutinizing gaze. I wish she'd just tell me to get the hell off her property and be done with it.

"I had a feeling you hadn't been entirely honest with me," she said slowly.

I cringed. So much for putting on a convincing act. "You did?"

"Yes." She sat her mug down, clasping her hands in front of her on the table. "And I'll be straight with you: I don't like dishonesty and I don't like being lied to. That being said, hearing your full story, I think I can better understand why you did what you did."

I shook my head. "It's not an excuse."

"It's not an excuse, no, but it does give me context that lets me understand why you would feel compelled to do something like lie about your background and your experience."

I blinked rapidly, not entirely certain where this conversation was even headed anymore.

"Like I said," Anita continued. "I'm not keen on the lying. But I can say that I've watched how hard you've worked and applied yourself these last few weeks. Don't think I haven't seen you in the tack room with those library books."

I flushed again, ducking my chin.

"I admire your dedication to learn. You don't have to know everything. Honestly, you're never going to know everything anyway. You made a mistake, but you've admitted it. And true, perhaps you could have done it sooner, but you *did* call the vet when you were in over your head. If I know what you know and what you don't know, I can help you fill in the gaps so there's not another incident like this weekend."

"You mean…" I bit my lower lip, daring to look her in the eye. "You mean I can stay?"

"Provided you agree that you will be honest with me from here on out. And if you're not, we'll have to revisit this conversation again. And I may not be so lenient the next time."

My chest fluttered and I was barely able to keep my jaw from dropping. I couldn't believe it.

"Yes," I said. "Yes, I promise I will be completely honest about everything. I swear."

"Good." Anita gave me a soft smile. "This afternoon, I want you to write down a list of all the things you learned how to do at your barn in Atlanta. I'll look over it tonight and we'll make a plan to fill in the gaps and get you caught up."

"Thank you. Thank you *so* much."

"You're very welcome. Now, I have to get unpacked before chores, but I'll see you down at the barn at four. And we'll get Winter with her meds together tonight."

"I'm going to go work on that list," I said as I got up from the table.

She saw me to the front door and as I made my way back down the hill back to the barn, my steps felt a little lighter. Anita was giving me a second chance. I wanted this job, wanted to learn from Anita and these horses. Taking the leap and coming to Virginia had been the best thing I'd ever done for myself. I had a future here; one I was going to do everything I could to keep. When I reached the bottom of the hill, I paused by the paddock fence. Winter was grazing along the fence line with Esperanza, the two mares dotted in golden beams with the setting sun. The quiet noise of the horses tearing and munching on grass was like its own little symphony.

"Hey, pretty girls," I said, leaning on the fence rails.

Esperanza flicked her ears at me and kept grazing, but Winter looked up. She walked over and put head over the fence, giving me a view of the antibiotic paste still coating the sides of her muzzle.

"Sorry I've been such a screwup," I told her, rubbing her cheek. "Anita is going to help with your meds tonight, so hopefully it'll go a lot easier. And hopefully you don't get hurt again. But if you do, next time, I'll know what to do."

The mare blew her breath into my face and I closed my eyes for a minute, taking in that distinct sweet smell of horse. She let me scratch her cheek a few minutes before she returned to Esperanza's side. The two mares ambled a bit farther down the fence line, side by side. I paused for a moment to watch them, basking in the quiet peace that seemed to come so easily at Heart and Soul. I might not have ever really had much of a home before, but I was going to make one here. Those roots I'd been missing for most of my life were wanting to stretch out and grow deep here in a way they'd never wanted to anywhere else. There wasn't any place else I wanted to be more than Heart and Soul Ranch.

82

Glossary of Equestrian Terms

- **Barefoot:** horses who do not wear any form of horse shoe.

- **Breeches:** snug fitting pants worn for riding.

- **Bute:** anti-inflammatory medication commonly used in horses.

- **Cavesson:** a type of bridle used in training. A traditional cavesson had three rings on the nose piece and is typically made of leather.

- **Crownpiece:** the top section of a halter or bridle that rests behind a horse's ears.

- **Cooler:** fleece blanket used to help cool down or dry off a sweaty horse in cold weather.

- **Curry comb:** rubber grooming tool used for brushing a horse.

- **Dressage:** meaning "to train". A form of equine gymnastics that, if applied with care, can be used to straighten and strengthen horses. Also a form of competitive riding.

- **Equine vet:** a vet who specializes in treating horses.

- **Gelding:** a castrated male horse.

- **Green horse:** a horse with limited or minimal training.

- **Grooming:** cleaning a horse with various brushes and tools. Always done before riding, but also done on a regular basis to check the horse for any signs of sickness or injury.

- **Groundwork:** working with a horse on the ground instead of on their back. Can be done in a variety of different ways, including on a lead line, at liberty, in-hand, ect.

- **Halter:** a piece of equipment that goes on a horse's head and allows the handler to lead and direct them.

- **Hunter:** a type of show horse that competes in jumping competitions that emphasize style and form.

- **Jumper:** a type of show horse that competes in jumping competitions that are judged on speed and accuracy.

- **Kissing spines:** a syndrome that affects the horse's spinal column and usually causes significant pain.

- **Large animal vet:** a vet who treats all farm animals, including horses.

- **Lead line:** a rope that is attached to a horse's halter. Can vary in length and can be used for every day handling or training.

- **Long lining:** a type of groundwork where two long lead lines are used, allowing the handler to be further away from, but still connected to, the horse.

- **Mare:** a female horse.

- **Martingale:** a piece of riding equipment that connects to the reins and limits how high a horse can raise its head.

- **Paddock boots:** ankle length leather boots used for riding and working around horses.

- **Rope halter:** a thinner type of halter, usually made of yachting braid rope, and used in training.

- **Shod:** horses who wear some form of horse shoe, usually metal.

- **SMZs:** antibiotic medication commonly used in horses.

- **Stiff brush:** stiff bristled brush used to groom horses.

- **Suspensory ligament:** ligament in the horse's lower leg.

If injured, can potentially end a horse's ridden career.

- **Tack:** equipment used for riding a horse, i.e. saddle, bridle, saddle pad, girth, ect.

- **Tacking up:** the process of putting tack on a horse to prepare them to be ridden.

- **Tall boots:** tight fitting leather boots that go up to the knee that are used for riding.

- **Topline:** referring to the muscles of the horse's back.

- **Untacking:** removing tack from a horse.

Acknowledgements

Thank you to my "barn moms": Rabiah, Elise, Kelly, and Kathy. Thank you for taking me under your wing as "one of your girls."

Thank you to Dr. Jessica Mattingly for looking over sections of this book to check for veterinary accuracy and for always being willing to answer questions.

Thank you to my husband for being the best horse dad ever by making sure our boys and the farm are taken care of, even when my health gets the better of me and I've got deadlines to meet. And for listening to my talk about the "fictional ponies" while working on this book.

Thank you to Rhapsody (believe me, I will never forget that splinter), Zuni, and WinterMix for providing some of the equine inspiration for this book.

Thank you to Susan & April for being willing to edit a "horse book." Y'all always make my manuscripts shine and challenge me as a writer.

Thank you to Natalie Keller Reinert and Linda Shantz for helping pave the way for the rest of us to write "horse books for adults."

And as always, thank you to my readers. Your support is what helps me continue to bring you more stories.

About The Author

Hannah E. Carey began telling stories as soon as she was old enough to talk and she hasn't stopped since. As a Dysautonomia warrior, writing and her love of stories allow her to explore new places & worlds, no matter what her body throws at her. She loves all things romance and writes romantic fantasy with fierce heroines that is inspired by her love of mythology, along with romantic women's fiction that stars loveable four-legged companions and is inspired by her years of being a horse & dog mom, her background in equine rescue, and her years of working as a certified Centered Riding Instructor. When she's not writing, you'll find her reading romance novels and spending time with her husband, horses, and dog on her small hobby farm.